7AR

Please return / renew by date
You can renew at:
norlink.norfolk.gov.uk
or by telephone: 0844 800 8006
Please have your library card & PIN ready.

I\c

£\

NORFOLK LIBRARY
AND INFORMATION SERVICE
NORFOLK ITEM

Cheated Hearts

Cheated Hearts

Jane McLoughlin

ROBERT HALE · LONDON

ISBN 978-0-7090-8418-1

Robert Hale Limited
Clerkenwell House
Clerkenwell Green
London EC1R 0HT

www.halebooks.com

2 4 6 8 10 9 7 5 3 1

Typeset in 11½/16pt Palatino
Printed and bound in Great Britain by
Biddles Limited, King's Lynn

1 The Country Mouse

What is so comforting about clichés that even quite intelligent people fall back on them in moments of stress? Lucy Drake was no exception. She tended to express her serious emotions in terms of ancient precept. In her case it was probably something to do with having a vicar for a father – or perhaps her way of coming to terms with feelings with which she wasn't sure she could cope. Anyway, on Friday night she repeatedly told herself, 'You can lead a horse to water but you can't make it drink'. Which seemed to sum up rather too exactly the state of her relationship with Paul. She called it her Friday feeling, but only to herself.

Things had been much the same most Friday nights since she'd met Paul Meyer, the man who was the love of her life. As usual everything was ready. The cassoulet had been cooking in the oven all afternoon and the wine had been breathing almost long enough to have a life of its own. The table was set, matches poised to light the candles. Only Paul was missing.

Nothing new about that, Lucy thought. Then she wondered what her friend Maxine would say on Monday morning when she told her that Paul had once again failed to arrive on a Friday night.

Maxine had no sympathy for Lucy or for anyone else who was prepared to turn down perfectly good Friday night dinner invitations with her friends in the village in favour of waiting in for someone from London who more often than not didn't turn up until next day, if at all. But then, according to Maxine, only men got away with such behaviour. Maxine saw all men as her enemies; she never had, and she never would, let any man ride roughshod over her.

Oh but, Max, you would, Lucy thought; you would if you got the chance. Poor Max. Lucy called her Max because it suited her and Maxine didn't. And Max/Maxine had had the nerve to call Lucy a freak.

Lucy thought this was a bit unfair from a friend. Particularly a friend whom most of the locals openly called a weirdo. Most of them thought that Max was lesbian. They didn't realize that her macho front masked her failure to fulfil her real nature as a mother-figure – she'd never met the right man. Poor old Max, Lucy thought, how sad to spend a whole lifetime in unwilling celibacy. No wonder she was odd.

All the same, Lucy knew that she'd really been miffed when Max called her a freak because deep down she suspected that without Paul she herself might one day be very much like Max.

She told herself that there was nothing odd about the way she was about Paul. It was perfectly natural, it was the way women were; millions of women undoubtedly sat around on Friday nights, like her, waiting for the sound of a car pulling up outside to set their lives alight for the next thirty-six hours or so, before bloody Sunday evening plunged them back into a dimmed existence of anticipating the next weekend. I can't be the only one to suffer the same madness, Lucy told herself.

She tried to imagine the implications of all those other women being psychologically disturbed like herself at any one time. It was mind-boggling. If half of the females aged between eighteen and thirty-five were deranged by love simultaneously, it was a scary proportion of the population all to be suffering temporary insanity at the same time. It should be a serious political issue, Lucy thought, no wonder politicians were so out of touch with real people.

She conceded, pouring a small tot of the practically gasping red wine to make herself feel better, that Max might even have a point, calling her freaky. Lucy didn't want to feel only half alive when Paul wasn't with her, she really didn't. Time and time again she'd told herself she wouldn't do it, she would not be so emotionally dependent on those few magic hours with him. She had tried to stop herself, but she couldn't. And she didn't want to. She'd spent long enough in a suspended state of benign monotony before she and Paul fell in love to know she'd much rather be riding life like a roller coaster, with highs and horrible lows, even if it did mean that she spent about seventy per cent of her time metaphorically in the pending tray.

The truth was that Lucy was incredibly, unbelievably, utterly happy because of Paul. And this state of euphoria had come totally out of the blue. It wasn't that she hadn't expected this wonderful thing called love would never happen to her: it was simply that she hadn't known that it could exist at all.

She'd had no precedents to study. Her mother had died when she was three and from then on her father, who was the village vicar, had never, apparently, given women a second thought. In Lucy's mind, people were either happily or unhappily married and happiness for a married woman seemed to have something to do with making jam and seeing that the children did their homework and the husbands went off to work by 8.15 every morning. The women who were unhappily married had jobs, complained about their children's behaviour, didn't like dogs, and seemed to spend their weekends wishing it was Monday. Lucy's poor friend Tara Burns was just such an unhappily married woman. Tara also illustrated another of Lucy's observations on the state of love, namely that happy women were mostly born and bred in a village, like the one in rural Devon where she lived, while women like Tara were incomers. Happy women *belonged* to the community: unhappy women were outsiders.

Lucy told herself, That's why I over-reacted to what Max said.

It frightened her to think that the way she felt about Paul might make her into an outsider in the rest of her life. She wanted Paul to be part of her life, but otherwise she didn't want that life to be different from the way it was before he came on the scene. Familiarity, she told herself, breeds content.

Since she'd met Paul, she'd spent most of the week in a state of disbelief at what had happened to her. Meeting him and falling in love seemed like a miracle. Then, most incredibly of all, he had fallen in love with her. If this marvel only became substantive fact at the weekend, well, so be it. Her weekday incredulity at her own good fortune wasn't just girlish modesty. She had no illusions about who and what she was, which was just about everything which would lead anyone with a healthy pinch of cynicism to rule out the slightest possibility that Paul Meyer could ever be interested in her.

For one thing, Paul was outstandingly attractive. He wasn't simply good-looking, which he was, but he had real charisma too. It was that sort of magnetic quality which drew people to him, often in spite of themselves. And his work made him even more glamorous because most people couldn't put their finger on what exactly he did, except it was something to do with show business. He seemed to be some sort of luminary in the record industry, close to all sorts of celebrities, a familiar face in all the best places to eat and drink and shop. And he drove a long, low, purple slitty-eyed sports car with a highly tuned engine which invariably choked in indignation when he tried to go anywhere through the narrow, winding country lanes where Lucy lived.

Lucy seemed his absolute opposite. She obviously never gave her appearance a second thought; her fair hair hung too long, loose and frizzy; she wore no make up and was a little too heavy for her height. She looked like a simple country bumpkin, a contented woman of thirty plus with a tabby cat and chickens. She was the sort of female who should have married at twenty-two and had lots of children and a farmer husband. But sadly it hadn't happened. Instead she had had to look after her father, who'd suffered from Alzheimer's for years before he died of pneumonia. That had been three years ago, and by then Lucy wasn't a girl any more, she'd turned into the kind of worthy but dull woman more likely to appeal to the family saloon sort of man than the sports car fanatic. If she listened to music, it was Classic FM; the only designer label she'd ever worn was Levi jeans and she'd never even seen Japanese food.

In the early days of her relationship with Paul, Lucy had been worried that he might think she was quite different from the way she really was. They'd met in London, in a wine bar in Covent Garden. She'd been waiting for Helen, an old friend from school who lived in Canonbury. Twice a year Lucy went up to London and waited in a bar for Helen to finish work. Then they'd go to a theatre together. Lucy usually stayed the night with Helen and caught the morning train back home to Devon the next day.

When she met Paul, the bar where Helen had arranged to meet her was crowded. He accidentally knocked over her drink and insisted on buying her another. They were still chatting when Lucy's mobile phone rang and Helen said she was held up at work and couldn't meet her.

So Paul took her to dinner. That was the start of it.

In spite of appearances, though, Lucy wasn't really a country cousin struggling to wrest an honest crust from the reluctant soil. She'd been brought up like that, on a vicar's pay. But Lucy's father was the second son of a minor aristocrat and when his bachelor elder brother had suddenly died twenty years ago, he had inherited the substantial family home a mile or so outside his isolated parish in rural Devon.

The house was already run down when Lucy and her father moved in. There was no real money to keep it up, and Lucy's father wouldn't consider betraying family tradition by selling it. He left it to Lucy when he died.

Of course his stipend had stopped at his death. Lucy was left to live on a very small private income and her earnings doing secretarial work two days a week for Tara's husband Quentin Burns. Quentin ran a small computer graphics business from home. There was scarcely enough work to fill those two days, so Lucy couldn't ask him to pay her more. She also earned a bit extra sewing curtains and doing upholstery repairs for the locals. She scraped a living. On paper, though, she was rich, a woman of property. But of course she couldn't sell the house for anything like what it was worth until she could afford to repair it, and she couldn't afford to repair it until she could sell it.

She didn't want to sell it in any case. It was where she belonged. Her happiest childhood memories were of the times she'd spent at the house before her uncle died. So, to make ends meet, every now and then she sold off one of the few remaining family treasures – a few good pieces of furniture and some old-fashioned ancestral jewellery. The money she raised in this way kept the place just about habitable, and she was able to put out of her mind the thought that anything would ever have to change by simply never going into most of the rooms in the house. But the sad truth was that most of the place was all but derelict: the roof leaked; fronds of virginia creeper had infiltrated two of the rooms on the second floor; and the sky was visible through a collapsed part of the roof in some of the others. In the room next to her bedroom on the first floor, Lucy could hear a pair of owls who were nesting there, snoring like drunken old men through the wall.

Lucy laughed at all this, and so did Paul. He said the state of the house was part of what she was. He loved her, he said, he loved her home, and he had plans of his own for the house.

'Once I can organize the business so I spend most of my time here with you in the country, I'll get all this sorted,' he said to her often as they lay together on a pile of cushions in front of the fire on a Sunday afternoon.

'Yes, I know you will,' she said, half asleep in his arms.

'You can tell me next week what you think we should do with it,' he said. It was his cue to get up and gather his scattered clothes to dress. 'Now I've got to get going, or I'll waste hours in the traffic.'

He said more or less the same thing every week. Lucy didn't take his promises about the house very seriously; but he gave her something to dream about in the interminable hours before the next Friday. All that week, she'd been planning a colour scheme for the dining room to tell him about over the cassoulet.

Suddenly, the telephone rang.

Paul sounded harassed. 'I've been held up,' he said. There was a lot of background noise, but Lucy recognized his busy-at-the-office voice so she tried to swallow her disappointment. In passing, she was glad she'd decided on the cassoulet rather than devilled prawns; cassoulet was often better reheated.

'I'll see you when I see you, then,' she said. She knew only too well that she mustn't let him hear how disappointed she was.

'As soon as I can make it,' Paul said.

'Love you,' Lucy said, but he had already rung off.

It didn't help that she'd been half expecting his call. It was always work. And as usual when this happened, Lucy thought of Maxine and she imagined she could hear her friend's scornful voice in her ear: 'Working my arse! He's not working, you idiot; he's married.'

He is, Lucy told herself, yes, he must be married. I've got to find out if he is.

She couldn't imagine why she had been avoiding the issue, except she was in love and she didn't want anything to ruin it.

Then she pulled herself together. Why should she take any notice of Max, Max who was an embittered spinster who just said things like that for the sake of it? People in the music business didn't work nine to five; it was much more likely that Paul was working than that he was married.

But secretly, for the first time, Lucy seriously wondered if Max could be right. It was possible. Of course it was.

Lucy didn't want to think about it. It made no difference. What mattered was that Paul wasn't on his way to be with her and, whatever the reason, it was a form of rejection. Paul was rejecting her. Max is right about one thing, Lucy told herself, I'm a freak; it can't be normal to feel as though the world has caved in because Paul might not be here until tomorrow.

Lucy felt bad because as long as he was safe, it made no difference if Paul had been held up by a train crash or a motorway pile-up or a bombing. All she cared about was that Friday night, probably Saturday morning, would be lopped off the brief few hours of holiday ending on Sunday afternoon. Eighteen hours or so to be added to the endless week. Her sane self would have known that the way she was behaving was scary; but she was in love, and no woman in love was altogether sane.

2 The Urban Fox

'Evening, Miss,' said Ted, the porter for the block of exclusive mansion flats behind Marylebone station where Sue Stockland lived on the top floor.

Ms Stockland, as she liked to be called, ran a successful public relations consultancy from her apartment. She was not impressed by Ted's familiarity.

'Too hot to wear your uniform jacket, Ted?' she asked in the special tone she had which sounded as though she was sucking an old-fashioned acid drop. Sue wasn't one to give up easily and it always annoyed her, given the amount it cost every one of the residents of that block of flats to employ him, that Ted didn't even try to look smart.

'It is hot tonight, isn't it, Miss,' he said with a smile that doubled as a sneer and Sue sighed. She knew that she wasn't going to get anywhere with him. If she really wanted to press the issue, she'd have to bring it up at the next freeholders' meeting. She thought she might do it. Apart from his general attitude, she thought it fairly pointless to pay good money for a security man who was on the puny side of flyweight.

As she opened the door of her flat, though, she thought Ted had a point. It was stifling inside. Paul must have closed all the windows before he left to drive west to the bucolic idyll where his dreary little wife dusted and polished and prepared dishes of earthy vegetables and bug-bitten fruit to welcome her hunter-gatherer back to the family fold. Usually it amused Sue that Paul felt it was his duty to his wretched kids to spend weekends with them, providing them with intellectual yeast to leaven his wifey's doughy conversation. Sue dismissed this obligation as nonsense, telling him they'd get more out of watching children's TV. He was serious about his fatherly duty, however. By some freakish genetic aberration, Paul and his wife had produced hyperactive geniuses as children. These two young boys, aged 12 and 14, turned destructive when they were bored. They were easily bored, too, particularly at weekends. Paul had to do what he could to channel all that nervous energy and excess brain-power. Sue took this to mean that he felt he owed it to them to spend time with them even if he didn't want to.

Sue kept to herself her personal impression that the children sounded to her as though they would both benefit from some healthy discipline and being told no for a change, but then, as Paul said, what did she know about kids?

Nothing, thought Sue, and thanked God for it.

All the same, kids apart, she felt uncomfortable when she considered how protective Paul plainly felt towards his wife. Sue thought perhaps he felt guilty because the woman was obviously so easy to deceive. Paul had his own telephone in the Marylebone flat which he and Sue shared during the week. Sometimes when he was out she heard his phone ringing and knew it was the wife because everyone else rang him on his mobile. Sue had to fight the temptation to pick it up and make Paul's wife aware that there was another woman in his life, a woman he was with because he loved her, not out of a sense of duty. Sue never did actually pick up the phone, though, because the wife was bound to say something to Paul and Sue suspected he would never forgive her if she blew the gaff. It wouldn't be how hurt the wife was that Paul would mind so much; what would anger him would be the way Sue's meddling would upset the carefully contrived balancing act of his life. So in spite of the temptation to tell the wife the truth, she was afraid of what

might happen if she forced the issue. He had a temper, she knew that. She couldn't quite forget the time she'd been with Paul driving through the Angel. An old woman in a Metro had stalled at the lights. Paul had exploded with anger. He'd jumped out of his precious purple Lotus and pulled the door of the Metro open, shouting at the old woman. Sue thought he was going to hit her. Since then, she'd been frightened of giving the violence inside him the chance to erupt.

Sue was afraid, too, that if she forced the wife issue, she could lose him. It upset her that Paul should be so bound to a woman who plainly had nothing more to offer him than that she looked after his children. Sue resented the sons who were such a problem to Paul and seemed to give him no pleasure. She thought he was stupid to put the effort and the money he did into people he didn't even seem to like very much. And they, at the same time, seemed to dislike him.

Once, she actually told him how she felt about this. He'd asked her to lend him five thousand pounds towards some course he said one of the kids needed. She'd asked Paul why he needed to borrow the money, he was a rich man. He'd given her a funny look and said that the best thing for the boys would be for him to divorce his wife and marry her so that she could provide a more stimulating maternal role model for them, so he wouldn't need to spend money on these courses. Sue didn't laugh; she thought he meant it. He sounded as though he did. But then he burst out laughing and she laughed too.

She gave him the money. After that, she didn't mention his sons again if she could help it. She had no doubt at all that she would much rather give Paul money than live with his children. She loved him and thought of the two of them as a long-term couple, but for her there could be no question of their marrying until the two hyperactive monsters had grown up and left home for good.

Sometimes Sue wondered what the wife was really like. She

tried to feel guilty about her. But why should I? she asked herself, I'm no threat to such a *hausfrau*. I don't want to have anything to do with what's between the two of them.

Sue was well aware that there was nothing romantic about what she had to give Paul. She didn't try to define it, but it had to do with her familiarity with the celebrity world which she had made her own domain. This gave her a kind of power among people who could make things happen for Paul. She gave him access to a milieu which otherwise he could never enter. She took this for granted. Oddly, she wasn't even curious about what Paul wanted from the contacts she gave him. She'd never tried to pin him down on how he made the considerable money he did. He'd told her when they first met that he was in business; she'd left it at that.

Anyone else she would have despised for needing her. He was very attractive though, and she enjoyed being with him. Ordinarily she wouldn't have got really involved, but she had with Paul. She'd fallen in love, really in love. Time and again she asked herself how she'd allowed this to happen, but the more she tried to analyse it, the more it seemed to be beyond her control. She felt helpless, which made her angry with herself. It was the first time she had loved for real; the first time she'd known the torment of emotional uncertainty. She suspected that she loved him more than he loved her. Knowing what he wanted from her gave her a slight hold over him. And it gave her a reason for continuing to compete hard in a business she was beginning to find tedious. Sometimes, when she was alone at weekends, in the flat where everything around her was a reminder of Paul, she thought how ironic it was that she had started to resent the demands of her profession only when she began to dream of a different life altogether with the man who loved her partly because of the world she worked in.

Sue wasn't used to being unsure of herself. She'd been on her own since she was seventeen, when her mother, Pat, went to live in Australia with a surfer from the Gold Coast. Pat never told her daughter who her father was. For a while, as a child, Sue had felt sorry for herself. When she got bored with that, she saw, suddenly, that there was nothing and no one to stop her creating the life she wanted for herself. She could do anything she liked. After that, she'd never looked back. She was beautiful, talented, respected. She ran her public relations business so successfully that she could almost make or break celebrity careers with a lift of her eyebrow.

How, she asked herself, could Paul's domestic drudge of a wife with her dreary coffee mornings and her old Laura Ashley flowered dresses and her silly chatter compete with that? If Sue ever felt guilty about the wife, she told herself that Paul would be much more discontented with the poor cow if it weren't for her. And, she thought, from everything he'd ever said about the woman, she deserved what had happened. Sue couldn't have seduced him if he hadn't been looking for – well, for a diversion, if not an escape.

Sue had been with Paul for two years. They'd met in Leicester Square at the London première of a Hollywood movie. Sue had been doing UK publicity for the American company. There was a party later at a Soho night club. Paul was there at the bar. She never wondered at the time how he'd got in. He caught her attention and they got into conversation. Then, in the first greenish light of a new day, they'd tottered up Shaftesbury Avenue looking for a cab. She took him home and then to bed.

And since then he'd spent most weekdays living with her at the flat.

Sue liked having the weekends to herself. She found the intensity of her relationship with Paul quite claustrophobic sometimes. She liked having a breathing space so she could realize how much she missed him.

So now that the flat was empty, she went through the rooms symbolically spreading her wings by opening all the windows and abusing Paul for his irritating obsessions with security. He never left a window open. The flat was five floors up and Ted was employed to screen strangers who came into the building. That seemed to Sue security enough.

She felt better once she'd got some cooler air into the place. That was in spite of the noise from a construction site somewhere near the tube station in Marylebone Road, which even drowned the constant din of traffic.

She poured a drink and kicked off her shoes so as not to mark the white leather sofa. Then she tried to concentrate on a consumer research report she needed to study for a meeting on Monday. But her attention kept straying to the shoes she'd taken off. They sat on the carpet like fat pet dogs. They were designer originals, but in spite of what they'd cost, they looked enormous. The sight of those grotesque shoes made Sue cringe. All the doubts about how Paul could really love her crowded back into her mind. Someone with such huge feet was a freak, no one could really love her. Sue took it for granted that generally she scored high on any female standard of attractiveness, but her hideous big feet spoiled everything. She had never got used to the let-down of walking into a room looking like a *Vogue* model and then feeling hundreds of pairs of eyes glued to her oversized shoes. It would never have crossed her mind that few people even noticed them. In the early days, she'd wanted to burst into tears, but gradually she got angry. She wished they could all be struck dead. She wanted to kill them then and there. She hated them.

Sue thought of Paul, who might at that very moment be looking at his frump of a wife with the thick ankles and hefty upper arms that Sue gave her in her imagination – along with thin greasy hair and unplucked eyebrows – and admiring her pig-trotter little feet. Sue was angry with him, then, because in spite of herself, she couldn't treat such thoughts with the contempt they deserved.

She reached over to her diary to check on the places she could go that evening. Three promotion parties, the launch of a new perfume, or the opening of an exclusive new gaming club. Then she rang Neville, her best friend, who lived on the floor below in the flat directly under hers. He understood the agony of giant feet. Neville was a fashion designer who sometimes made use of her PR skills, and in return he gave her exquisite long tailored dresses which only hinted at the fact that she had feet at all. And at weekends, he took her to the sort of places such dresses demanded to be worn. And when he sang an old 1940s black American song 'I'd love to love you but your feet's too big' she actually laughed and only wanted to kill him a little.

'We're young, we're rich, we're beautiful, let's party,' Sue said as soon as he answered the phone.

Neville squealed with delight. 'Somewhere where the lights aren't too harsh, though,' he said. 'I'm overdue a date with the Botox lady.'

'I'll let you choose,' Sue said. 'I'm in a Monroe-ish mood myself.'

'She had big feet and knock knees, didn't she?' Neville said. 'I bet she never let them get in the way of a good time.'

Neville, I love you, she thought, I don't have to say a word and you know what I'm thinking. And then she thought, thank God he's gay, it's like having a sister without the sibling rivalry.

3 Underworld

In a cramped and overheated room four floors above an alley off Frith Street where at night drunken yobs screwed bored whores against the slimy walls, two men faced each other across a paper-strewn desk.

'You know what you've got to do?' the taller of the two men asked. He had a boxer's flattened nose and beetle brows that were at odds with the immaculate pin-stripe suit he wore.

The other, shorter but almost as broad as he was tall, nodded. Wearing only a T-shirt and dirty denim shorts, he looked like a primitive work of art, all his exposed skin glowing with brightly-coloured tattoos. As he moved his head, an ornate dragon tattooed on his bull neck reared its head, ready to blow flames.

'I don't want the bastard telling tales afterwards,' the first man said.

The single window in the room was caked with decades of London grime and hardly let in any light. A single electric bulb blurred with dust cast a dim glow above the two men, distorting their features so that they both seemed like shadows.

'You trying to tell me 'ow I do my job?' the man with the dragon tattoo muttered. His clenched hands looked like blocks of coloured marble decorating the desktop.

The first man opened a drawer in the desk and took out a roll of banknotes which he tossed towards the tattooed man.

'Persuade him to pay me what he owes and you'll get the rest,' he said.

'How long's 'e got to come up with it?'

'He's run out of time,' the first man said. 'His money or his balls, right?'

Both men laughed.

'You got a mug shot? I want to get the right guy. We don't want one of them tragic miscarriages of justice we read about in the newspapers, ain't that the truth?'

The man in the expensive pin-stripe suit opened another drawer and took out a bunch of photographs. He held them like a deck of cards to sort through them, then handed one to the tattooed man.

'He doesn't look like much,' he said. 'But he's a slippery bastard.'

'Why's 'e look like that?'

'Like what?'

'Like 'e's in a panto or summat. What's 'is line?'

'He owes me money, that's all.'

'No,' the tattooed man said, 'I mean, where'll I look for 'im?'

The other man shrugged. 'There's a club in Greek Street he drinks in, the *Hell Hole*. And he's got some sort of office above a sandwich bar behind Tottenham Court Road tube station. He doesn't seem to be spending much time there recently, though. My boys camped out for days waiting for him, but he didn't show.'

''E knows yer on to 'im, then?'

'Maybe, maybe not. He's a fool to himself.'

'Don't these suckers never learn?'

'You'd better hope they never do, or that'd be you out of a job.'

The tattooed man smiled and it was clear why he didn't do it often. He had no teeth.

The other looked startled.

'You'd better not let the mark see you like that. He won't come across if he thinks you're only going to suck him to death.'

'That's where you're wrong, you see,' the tattooed man said

with an air of resignation at the ignorance of his employer. 'They take me for a sucker …' he guffawed at his own wit '… they're off guard and then they learn that in my business there's not so much call for teeth as a deadly weapon.'

'I don't care how you do it,' the man in the pin-stripe suit said, 'as long as you do what I'm paying you for. I want my money and I want him dead, understand?'

'Oh, I got yer. 'You want the geezer wiped, right?'

'That's about the size of it, yes,' the man in the pin-stripe suit said.

4 The Lover

Lucy waited up for Paul until it was so late that she began to fear one of her neighbours would see the light on in the house and come to check that she was not being robbed or attacked. People who lived in villages did kind things like that, or, at least, Lucy liked to think they did. So she went to bed and – surprisingly – to sleep. She dreamed that Paul had arrived with a pregnant woman who was, he said, his wife whom he loved so much that he wouldn't ever be seeing Lucy again. In her sleep Lucy kept telling herself she was dreaming and trying to wake up, but she couldn't.

The sound of Paul's car tyres on the gravel of the drive woke her early next morning.

He looked terrible. He followed her into the kitchen while she made coffee, hardly speaking. He sat slumped at the kitchen table like a sack of corn with the grain leaking out of it. For a moment, as she brought him coffee, she thought he had fallen asleep, but he opened his eyes and tried to smile at her as she put the mug in front of him.

'What is it, Paul?' she asked. 'Something's happened, hasn't it?'

'No, no of course not, there's nothing wrong,' he said, but even he sounded doubtful.

Lucy waited until he had drunk the coffee before she asked him anything more.

Then she said, 'You can tell me, you know. I want to help. We're a couple. Or do you think I'm nagging you?'

She stepped back, afraid he might resent her questioning. Lucy knew little about men except, perhaps, rather too much about old men like her father. And of course there was Tara's husband, Quentin, but he was her boss and the only thing they ever talked about when they were alone was work and even those conversations were restricted to the tedious administrative side of the business which was what she dealt with. She didn't ask him questions, anyway; he told her what to do. Her experience of men as emotional creatures was gleaned entirely from watching old films on television with her father before he died. He'd loved those old films, although he'd had trouble keeping awake during them.

So she felt daunted at asking Paul direct questions and pushing for straight answers.

'I want to tell you,' he said. 'You're the only person in the world who might understand. My God, if you only knew how often I've wanted to come clean.' He covered Lucy's hand with his and seemed about to say something momentous. But he turned away. 'It's no good,' he said, 'I can't.'

'You've got to tell me,' she said, 'a trouble shared is a trouble halved. And anything's better than not knowing.'

He looked doubtful. Then he said, 'I feel terrible that I didn't tell you before, Lucy. So many times I've wanted to, but we were so happy together, I couldn't bear to spoil it. I couldn't bear it if I drove you away. I need you so much.'

Lucy started to say something, but he went on. 'Nothing I'm going to tell you makes any difference to one thing, which is that I love you and that you're the only woman I've ever really loved. Oh, Lucy, I couldn't bear to lose you.'

Lucy heard a chilling little voice somewhere in the back of her mind saying, 'Max was right, he *is* married.'

He buried his face in his hands. She thought he was going to weep, and she went cold with fear. She had no idea what she should do or say in the face of such distress.

She pulled up a chair and sat down beside him. Shyly she took his hand and pulled it away from his face as she tried to make him look her in the eye. 'Paul, you've got to tell me,' she said. 'You're not going to lose me whatever happens. What is it? Are you married?'

He looked startled. She thought he seemed relieved but then he touched her cheek and sighed. 'I wish it were that simple,' he said, and she was frightened at the sadness in his voice. 'Yes, I'm married, but that's not the problem.'

Lucy's first thought was of Maxine. She felt grateful to her. Max is a true friend, she thought, she tried to tell me, she wanted to warn me. 'Of course he's married,' Max had said. But how did she know what Lucy hadn't even guessed?

It was as though she'd only heard part of what he said. She stopped listening when he said 'I'm married', and she was glad because he was so dismissive of it. It didn't seem to matter much to him. 'Why didn't you tell me?' she asked quietly.

Paul looked away, unable to meet her eyes. 'Oh, Lucy,' he said, 'it sounds like such a cliché, but I was afraid you wouldn't understand. My marriage was over long before we met, it was a sham. I haven't thought of myself as a married man for years. I never loved my wife, and she didn't love me. But I'm tied to her by something much stronger than marriage vows.'

Incongruously, Lucy thought of Mr Rochester in *Jane Eyre*. But this wasn't a book, she told herself, this is really happening. 'You've got to tell me, Paul,' she said. 'What is it?'

He hesitated, then started to talk in a quick, breathless monotone as though he were reading the words from a script he had been trying to learn by heart.

'I have a daughter. Her name is Julie. Julie was born with a genetic defect. Her mother can't cope, that's why I'm there with her all week. There's nothing between us, but I could never abandon her because of Julie.'

Before he had finished speaking, Lucy had put her arms around him and held him close.

'Paul, it's all right, of course I understand. Poor little girl, little Julie, of course you can't leave, she needs you.'

Paul pulled away. He blew his nose. 'We will be together one day, Lucy, but now you see why I can't even wish for it because our happiness would mean Julie was dead. The doctors say she hasn't very long to live. Children like her usually die in their teens. At best she's got eight or ten years.'

It seemed to Lucy that she had never heard Paul talk like this before. Usually he was practically monosyllabic about anything to do with emotion. He must have been going over and over in his mind how he could put his deepest feelings into words like this.

'Isn't there anything they can do?' she said. 'The doctors, I mean. They're making amazing advances....'

Paul shook his head. Lucy heard him stifle a sob. 'That's what makes it worse,' he said. 'There's a medical team at a hospital in America where they've treated some children with Julie's condition and in a few cases they seem to have stopped the process of degeneration. If they develop this treatment, it may help these children in future, but I'm afraid it will come too late for Julie.'

Lucy jumped to her feet. 'No,' she said, 'you can't give up like this. You've got to send her there. You've got to get her that treatment.'

'Darling, don't you think I've looked into it?' Paul said. 'That's why I was held up last night, making contact with the experts in Los Angeles. To get them at work I had to call in the middle of the night because of the time difference, but I did have a long talk with them. Lucy, they told me how much it would cost. I can't raise anything like enough.'

'Is it only the money? Could they take her? Could she get the treatment if you had the money?'

Paul put his head in his hands. She had to strain to hear him say a muffled, 'Yes'.

There was a long silence. Lucy took their empty coffee mugs

to the Aga and refilled them from the percolator keeping warm on the hotplate.

'I'll get you the money,' she said.

She kept her back to him. She didn't want him to be able to tell from her face how much of a personal sacrifice what she had just said would mean to her.

She said again, 'I'll get you the money.'

She heard Paul catch his breath. Then, in a voice full of longing, he said, 'No, Lucy, I couldn't take your money, I couldn't. Don't think I don't love you for offering, but I couldn't. I can't promise I could ever repay you.'

She took the filled mugs of coffee back to the table and sat beside him. 'I'm not talking about a loan, Paul. And I'm not giving the money to you; I'm giving it to Julie. She's your daughter and one day when you and I are together, she'll be my family, too. You can't refuse to let me do this.'

'But ...' He broke off, looking embarrassed, then went on in the tone of someone talking to a child. 'Lucy, my love, you don't realize the sort of money we're talking about. It's a wonderful gesture and I love you for it, but it's going to take more than selling a few pieces of family jewellery to get anywhere near what this would cost.'

Lucy took a deep breath. Am I mad? she asked herself. What would Max say? Then she thought, It doesn't matter what Max thinks, I decided to do it the moment Paul told me about Julie. There was nothing to think about.

'I can get the money,' she said. 'I'll sell the house.'

Paul stared at her. 'No,' he said, 'no, you can't. This is your family home, I can't ask you to give that up.'

'You can't count the family home against saving Julie's life? And you didn't ask me to do this, did you? I've told you this is what I want to do and you can't stop me. I want to do it. I'm going to ring the agent now.'

'But it's Saturday,' Paul said. 'There won't be anyone there. At least think about what you're doing and then you can ring on Monday, if you still want to go ahead.'

'I don't believe in second thoughts,' Lucy said. 'And no estate agent worth his salt's going to be closed on a Saturday.'

She smiled and kissed him lightly on the forehead as she got up to go through to the hall to look up the number of a local agent. When she kissed him she noticed he was sweating and she felt she had an inkling of how desperate he had been.

This means everything to him, she told herself.

And then, when she had made her call and fixed an appointment for the estate agent to meet her at the house on Monday, she stood at the hall window looking across the lawn towards the park full of trees planted by her ancestors before she went back to Paul to tell him what she had done.

She expected to feel that there was something to celebrate, but her action seemed detached from her. She asked herself, Why does this feel like an anticlimax? Then she thought, What have I done?

5 It's Only Money

Sue was in the shower when the phone rang early on Monday morning. The connection was bad and she strained to hear. 'It's Paul. Something's come up.'

'I love you too and I'm counting the hours till I see you tonight,' she said.

'There's a complication,' Paul said.

'Meaning you won't be home tonight?'

Sue sounded terser than she'd intended, but her wet hair was dripping on the inlaid mahogany surface of the telephone table.

'No, nothing like that.' Paul dropped his voice to a whisper, 'I can't keep away from you, you know that.'

'OK. You're being overheard, is that what you're saying?'

'Something like that.'

'So you will be home tonight, so why are you calling?'

'Is this a bad time to talk?'

Sue was irritated and made no attempt to hide it. 'I can't see why you don't tell me whatever you want to say when you get home,' she said. 'I was in the shower and I'm soaking wet.'

'Sounds good to me,' Paul said. 'I've got a problem, though. I need money.'

'Go to the bank,' Sue said.

'I'm serious,' Paul said. 'It would be a loan. I can pay you back by next week, or the week after at the latest.'

Sue was shocked because he sounded so serious. She was used to lending him money to tide him over, there was the £5,000 and other much smaller sums, but he had never asked her over the phone like this and so formally. His voice had an unfamiliar, raw quality which surprised her, it made her think he was under unusual pressure.

She said slowly, trying to sound calm, 'There's nothing in the flat, but I suppose I could get it for you later. How much do you want?'

'Twenty thousand would do it for now?'

'Twenty thousand!' Sue couldn't believe she had heard right. She thought, If there's someone his end trying to listen to this call, they must have heard me screech. 'I can't get my hands on that kind of money at such short notice,' she said more quietly. 'Is this something for one of your kids?'

'There's been a bit of a panic here this weekend,' he said in an urgent whisper. 'My wife's threatened to walk out on everything if I don't get the boys on a residential course she wants them to do. She means it. Please, Sue, I wouldn't ask if I wasn't desperate, but if you don't help, I don't see what else I can do, I'll have to bring the boys up with me now and we'll have to put them up for a while.'

Sue took several deep breaths. 'She's calling your bluff,' she said. 'She couldn't do it, she's much too much of a doormat to walk out.'

'I thought that too,' Paul said, 'but I don't think she's bluffing. She's completely lost it this time; she might do anything.' Then he added in a conspiratorial whisper, 'Honestly, I'm afraid to leave them alone with her, the way she is.'

'Oh, God,' Sue said, 'I can't believe I'm doing this. You've got to get out of there, she could attack you or something. Tell her I'll have ten thousand for her tonight and you can get it to her tomorrow. See if she'll take that, and if not, I'll get her the rest in the next two days. Tell her anything, Paul, but for God's sake stop her doing anything stupid.'

'I'll try,' Paul said, but he did not sound confident.

Sue imagined what it would be like to have two churlish, bored teenage boys living in her beautiful bijou flat. That was bad enough, but this was also her office, it was no place for children. She quailed at the vision of coming back from work to find Paul and his sons making themselves at home in her sitting-room.

'Paul,' she said urgently, 'I'll be busy with a client tonight. Don't come back here, meet me about 10 at the *Hell Hole*.'

'I owe you,' Paul said. She'd said 'Love you back' before she realized he hadn't said, 'I love you'.

The detached sound of the dialling tone made her aware of how cold she was.

'You bet you owe me,' she said into the indifferent receiver, 'and I'm not going to let you forget it.'

The phone rang again as she put it down. For a moment, Sue was tempted to let it ring. She wasn't dripping any more, but she was shivering with cold. She would also have to wash her hair again if she wasn't going to look like a walking haystack.

She picked up the phone. She expected it to be Paul saying that his wife had backed down and that there was no need after all to find such a huge sum of money. The woman was apparently a manipulative bitch, but that didn't quite square with what Sue knew about her as the downtrodden, stupid drudge. Lots of victimized women were like that, Sue thought, but she'd never thought of Paul's wife as one of the scheming bitch types. She must have underestimated the cow. But then she told herself, No, this must be one of Paul's little games. She'd thought all along he was setting her some sort of test to reassure himself that she still loved him. She didn't know whether she should be pleased that he cared so much, or irritated by a reminder of the fact that he knew she loved him more than he loved her. Except he didn't know that, she thought, she'd made sure she never let him guess that. He still thought he was the one who was afraid of losing her, who thought he wasn't really good enough for her. As far as he's concerned, nothing's changed, she told herself.

But the balance of their relationship had changed, she knew it. Now she didn't want to tell him how much she loved him because she didn't want him to know how much power he had over her.

But it wasn't Paul on the phone. The new caller did not give her a chance even to ask who he was. He sounded hysterical. It took her some time to identify him as a new client, potentially an important one, an Estonian businessman who was negotiating to extend his established Eastern European holiday airline to fly commercial routes from a Northern English airport. Still naked from the shower and blue with cold, she had to pull herself together and deal with this before it turned into a crisis.

Something had gone wrong. Sue's client was impatient with local bureaucracy. He'd decided to ignore some regulation he saw as petty, and he'd taken action which now threatened to bring his business to a halt. The unions were involved. Sue had a vision of the months of work she had put in on setting up the deal disintegrating beyond repair.

Oh, God, she thought, listening to her client's guttural tirade reverberating like drums in her head. Silently, she cursed Neville, because he had recommended her to this crazy Estonian, who was the brother of one of Neville's former best friends.

'Shut up,' she shouted, 'shut up and listen.'

There was an astonished silence.

'Do nothing,' she said. 'You hear me, do nothing. I'm coming to you.'

The torrent of words started again. Sue lost her temper.

'Quiet,' she yelled. Then, less loudly but in the firmest tone she could manage, she said, 'There's a flight to Manchester which arrives at lunchtime. Meet me at the airport with your car and we'll sort this out.'

'What time lunchtime?' Her client sounded sulky. She knew she had won this round.

'Get your secretary to look it up,' she said, and put the phone down.

Damn, she said to herself. What about Paul and his money?

She tried to ring his mobile but it was turned off. She thought of dialling 1471 for the number he had called her from, but of course the Estonian ringing had wiped that. She would just have to keep trying his mobile.

That cow of a wife will just have to wait until I get back to London, she thought, that's the best I can do.

She dressed as quickly as she could and called a cab to take her to the airport. There she bought a ticket for the last seat on the plane to Manchester and had to sprint the final hundred yards to make the flight before the cabin staff closed the doors.

But her Estonian client was not at Manchester Airport to meet her. She rang his office and spoke to his secretary. He had gone to meet her at Leeds/Bradford. The secretary sounded disapproving, convinced that Sue must have given her boss the wrong information. At first she insisted there was nothing she could do to contact the irate Estonian. Sue realized that the girl was scared to act on her own initiative, afraid she would be blamed for the mix-up.

'You've got to contact him,' Sue said. 'He's bound to have his mobile. Tell him it's my fault, tell him anything you like, but it's very important we move quickly if this whole deal isn't going to go pear-shaped.'

'If you'd get off the line, he's probably trying to ring me,' the secretary said. 'I'll tell him when he calls.'

'You're a lot braver than I am, then,' Sue said. 'When he finds out you didn't move heaven and earth to put this mess right, he's going to blame you for everything that happens. And ...' she said with all the venom she could muster '... so will I.'

Reluctantly, the secretary rang her boss on his mobile on another line while Sue held on to hear where he wanted to meet her. She could hear his infuriated torrent of abuse before the secretary came back to her. She should take a taxi from the airport and they would meet on site as soon as she got there.

'Marvellous,' Sue said, 'it's miles away, it'll cost a fortune, and I haven't even had time to get to a cash machine. I hope Manchester taxis take credit cards.'

'Fat chance,' the secretary said. She sounded pleased.

Why do women like that always dislike me? she asked herself, and couldn't be bothered to try to think of an answer.

Then she thought about the money for Paul. After all, she told herself, it's only money.

She couldn't believe she'd thought such a thing.

6 A New Start

The house agent had not been encouraging at first. He was a very beautifully dressed young man in a pale linen suit with a silk bow tie, and chamois leather driving gloves. He was new to the area and he clearly expected to be valuing a stately home with a butler to open the door and sherry served in antique crystal from a wrought Jacobean silver salver before the light family lunch he would surely be invited to share.

He took Lucy for the maid. He actually asked for the mistress of the house.

'Yes,' Lucy said, holding out her hand, 'I suppose you could call me that.'

The agent looked as though he might faint. He mopped his brow with a silk handkerchief which matched his bow tie as he followed Lucy into the house and through the dilapidated hall to the drawing-room, where the ceiling sagged in swags like drapery.

'What kind of buyer are you expecting for this place?' he asked, sounding breathless.

'A rich one,' Lucy said.

'I foresee difficulties here,' the agent said. 'I'm confused about what you have in mind.'

'What I have in mind is to sell it for the best price I can get,' Lucy said. 'Needs must when the devil drives. And it would be nice if you, the person who is paid – highly paid – to be an expert in selling property, pulled out his finger and told me the answers to questions like that. How do I know what I have in mind till you tell me what the options might be?'

It was out of character for Lucy to talk like this but the situation was new to her, and it was bad enough to be actually putting her family home on the market without this poncy little beast making her feel ashamed of the poor old place.

'Some people would say it would be better to knock it down and start again,' the estate agent said.

'Some people might say that, if they were very stupid and had no sense of history,' Lucy said, 'but of course you wouldn't say something like that yourself, would you?'

Lucy looked at the agent and suddenly she was seeing her old home through his eyes. The house was derelict; the plaster was falling down, the paper peeling from the walls, it felt stone-cold and the smell of damp pervaded some of the rooms, one of which, up on the third floor, had a Russian vine growing through the outside wall and across the floor.

All the fight went out of her. She didn't want to put him off. His supercilious manner had made her act out of character, while she had been driven by the thought that she was doing this to save Paul's daughter's life. Now she had to fight back tears.

'Please,' she said, 'I've got to sell it. And there's no money to do anything to it. You've got to help me.'

The estate agent looked at Lucy, bundled up in her baggy cords and woollen hat. To him, she looked like the pupa of a large species of decorative butterfly who'd never been able to break out of her cocoon in that chill, dark, vault of a house. He sighed and put aside all thought of the taste of gracious living he'd been expecting.

'Do you have something I could pull on over these clothes,' he said with a resigned sigh. 'I don't seem to be dressed for this.'

Lucy gave him an old coat of her father's and a pair of

gumboots into which he could tuck his incongruous pale trousers.

'Right,' he said, 'where do you suggest we start.'

'I'm going to make us both a coffee and then leave you to get on with it.' Lucy said. 'I think it's best. I'd inhibit you, and you might end up trying to spare my feelings.'

The agent looked relieved. 'You sure?'

'Yes,' Lucy said. 'Do what you have to do, but remember I want a quick sale. I know it goes against your practice, but it's not a question of getting the best possible price. I want a quick sale and no waiting for chains or looking for mortgages.'

The agent seemed about to say something, possibly that no lender would give a mortgage on this house, but Lucy cut him short. 'Look on the bright side,' she said, and smiled sweetly at him. 'Two per cent of anything is better than two per cent of nothing. If I don't sell it at once, I won't sell it at all.'

In spite of himself, the agent smiled back. He was thinking that this woman had a really charming smile. And if she sold this pile, she might be looking for somewhere else to buy. There was a house on the books in the village nearby, a thatched cottage in a secluded lane by the church, with a stream in the garden and ducks in the pond on a small village green. He actually had a romantic image of Lucy there. He could see her tending summer window-boxes and doing her shopping on an old bicycle with a wicker basket on the handlebars. She was a good-looking woman, he could see that now. He might even call in when she was all settled in the cottage and have cream tea with her from time to time when he was in the area.

Lucy sat in the kitchen while the agent did his tour of the house. She wished she could have taken her coffee out into the garden, but in an east wind it was even colder outside than it was in. She tried to ignore the sounds of the agent moving around, thumps and bangs and the occasional exclamatory yelp.

At least he's getting a new definition of the wow factor, she told herself, but she couldn't even make herself smile.

She had to keep telling herself why she was doing this. I should be happy, she thought, this is for Paul and his poor little girl and it's the best possible cause.

But she looked round the familiar kitchen with the old-fashioned free-standing cupboards and the table bleached with scrubbing and the old Aga in the inglenook and the ancient flagged floor and the stable-door on to the yard and she fought hard not to cry. She tried to see the place through the agent's eyes, with the stained enamel sink and the wooden draining boards and the peeling walls, and she imagined how it would look after some modern young couple with plenty of money got hold of it and gutted and redesigned it with fitted units, all stainless steel and the latest electrical appliances giving the place a faceless look.

'It's worth it,' she said aloud, thinking of why Paul needed the money, 'it's in the best possible cause. Even Dad would think so.'

She heard the agent call her name from the hall. She wiped her eyes with the sleeve of her jumper and went to meet him.

'Well,' she said, 'what's it worth?'

The agent was about to make his standard little joke, 'Do you want the bad news or the worse news first?' but he looked at her and she knew he could tell she had been crying.

'Straight up,' he said, 'I can sell the place for conversion into apartments, a speculator on the books might take it to knock it down and develop the site. Planning permission's much easier than on green field land. Is it listed?'

'No, thank God. The original Elizabethan house was burned down in the nineteenth century and rebuilt. It's nothing special architecturally, and we were never one of the great aristocratic families. How much?'

She was astonished at the sum he mentioned and, at the same time, she was disappointed. For ages, the newspapers and television had been going on about soaring house prices, she'd half hoped the house might sell well enough to pay for Julie's treatment and leave something over so she could buy herself a little place to live. But she'd also feared that the house might be unsaleable, too far gone for even the greediest speculator to consider.

There would probably not be enough left over after Julie's treatment for Lucy to buy herself even a little flat. I can rent, she told herself, rent something somewhere and get a full-time job and earn a living. It's bound to bring me closer to Paul. I'll be part of him and Julie, not on the outside any more. It'll be a new start.

And anywhere she went would only be temporary, after all. Once Julie was cured, there was nothing to stop all three of them living together as a family. Even if Julie wanted to stay with her mother, Lucy thought, there would be nothing to stop Paul and her setting up a home together where Paul could spend weekends with his daughter.

Lucy, afraid she was getting carried away, brought her attention back to what the agent was saying.

'As I said, I've someone in mind who might be interested,' he said. He added, 'Given the particular circumstances of this sale.'

That means he'll sell it way under value and take a commission from the buyer, Lucy told herself.

The agent seemed to know what she was thinking. He shuffled his feet and said, 'That's if you really mean what you say about wanting the money quickly. If you're having second thoughts about that, I could probably get another fifty thousand, but it might take months.'

'Sell it,' Lucy said, 'sell it now.'

She walked with the agent to his car. And then, when she had watched him drive away, she turned back to look at the house. She was surprised that already something in her attitude to it had changed. It seemed no longer to have anything to do with her, and she was glad. A weight seemed to have been lifted from her. She'd expected to be overwhelmed by guilt and the accumulated disapproval of generations of her ancestors who had seen staying on in the place as some kind of sacred trust. She felt nothing of the sort. What she felt was a stirring of excitement.

For the first time in my life, she thought, I'm making a new start of my own, not one forced on me by Dad, or circumstances, or duty to a family I never knew. This time it's down to me.

Lucy smiled at the house. She had never really noticed the Victorian ugliness of it before, the gables like disapproving raised eyebrows; the windows, reflecting the overgrown laurels screening the road, seeming to frown; the red brick frontage promising always only an irascible welcome. She ran back through the open front door. I must ring Paul, she thought, to tell him the good news.

7 An Unlikely Confidante

By 9.30 that evening, it was clear that Sue would have to stay overnight in a hotel to sort out the details of the Estonian's deal in the morning.

People didn't have to know Sue very well to realize she was not the kind of woman to whom the prospect of a night out in any benighted northern town with this Estonian would appeal. Her Eastern European client's main sources of entertainment in England were premiership football and drinking, preferably simultaneously. She insisted on returning to Manchester and booked into a hotel in the city centre.

The hotel was a purely functional place without any frills, but Sue didn't care. She didn't want to spend money on luxury when she'd be leaving first thing in the morning.

In her room she kicked off her shoes, which were pinching so much after all the walking she had done that day that her toes were numb. But the sight of her feet was so depressing that she preferred to endure the pain and, after a struggle, got the shoes back on.

Then she rang Paul. She hoped he wouldn't try to remonstrate with her because, tired and hungry and frustrated with the way her meetings had gone, she was in the mood to explode whatever he said to her. She wanted someone to blame for her frustrating day. At the same time, she felt guilty that she had let him down about the money. She told herself it couldn't have been easy for him to ask any woman, even her, for so much. It must have been desperately important to him. She thought of him waiting in vain for her to meet him in the Greek Street club and she felt guilty, which made her all the more inclined to pick a fight with him.

When he didn't answer her call, she left a message on his mobile, then, as a last resort, rang his telephone at the flat. Amazingly, it seemed to her, she hadn't done this before. Only his wife rang that phone. It occurred to her that perhaps she was afraid to hear something special in his tone of voice when he thought he was talking to the wife. Any hint of affection or close-ness, and Sue would no longer be able to be sure that Paul was really as uninterested in the woman as he pretended.

This is insane, she told herself, he's got to keep the cow sweet, he's not going to let her know how much he hates her.

So she listened to the ringing tone and wished she were there in her own comfortable sitting-room, watching television and drinking a glass of good red wine.

But Paul did not answer. Sue left another message and decided that she needed to eat and have a drink before she did anything else.

It was late. She wanted something to take her out of herself, something to help her escape the day she'd had. The thought of room service and an evening staring at the magnolia walls and bland pictures of sailing scenes on a sunny summer day seemed too depressing to bear.

She had to go out, even if it was only to walk around the streets and drop into a late-night bar where she might get them to make her a sandwich.

On her way out of the hotel, she asked the hall porter if he could suggest somewhere she could go to unwind for an hour or two.

He looked doubtful. 'You want to be careful out alone this time of night,' he said. He was trying to be kind. 'The pubs can get rough even round here for a young lady on her own.'

'I don't want a pub,' she said. 'There must be a quiet club somewhere I could have a relaxing drink.'

'There's the *Fedora*, that's only a few hundred yards up the road,' he said.

'What's that?'

'It's a club, quite exclusive. A lot of our business guests like to round off the evening there when they're in town.'

'Do you have to be a member?'

The hall porter took a card from behind his desk. 'We have an arrangement with the management,' he said. 'This gives you temporary membership while you're staying here.'

'Thanks,' Sue said. She took the card and tipped him.

'Turn right out of here and walk towards a big department store you'll see ahead of you. Before you get to it, there's a little street on the right. The club's up there. You'll see the sign lighted up ahead of you, an outline of a bullfighter wearing one of those Spanish hats.'

'Thank you.'

'Enjoy your evening,' he said.

Sue felt very conscious of being alone as she turned out of the hotel lobby. She imagined she could feel the porter's eyes watching her as she walked away. She thought, He's probably wondering what's wrong with me, all on my own. He's pitying me. And then she told herself: he probably thinks I'm going out on the pull.

She found the club without trouble. As she walked up the pavement towards the red-lighted neon outline of the Spanish *señor*, she heard the sound of music coming from somewhere under her feet.

The *Fedora* was almost empty. A flamenco guitarist strummed softly from the back of a small stage and at the front a dark-haired girl in black fishnet tights and a basque of red and black satin danced in a desultory fashion around a painted pole. She had a crimson flower in her hair, but whether a gardenia or a rose it was hard to tell – the silk petals drooped so shapelessly. She was making no impression on a small group of men in suits sitting at a table near the stage. They were having some sort of argument. Sue, sitting on a stool at a small bar in the corner beside the stage, tried to listen to what they were saying, but she couldn't even make out the subject under discussion, so technical was their jargon.

She ordered a bottle of wine from behind the bar. Sue thought, as she waited for the bottle to be uncorked, that the barmaid in front of her wouldn't do much to attract the punters. She had been good-looking once, clearly, but now she looked older than she probably was.

The sight of the woman depressed Sue. She felt herself threatened physically by time. What she gave Paul depended on youth and glamour and an endless supply of energy which could be as easily turned on as a light bulb. Not so long ago this ageing barmaid must have felt like me, Sue thought, but now even the middle-aged drunken creeps who come in here would run a mile from her rather than screw her.

Sue knew she was becoming maudlin. She hated to feel alone like this. She was full of self-pity. All I want is someone to talk to about any old thing that comes into my head, just to take my mind off everything else, she told herself, and felt tears streak her face as she finished the bottle.

The dancer in the red and black basque gave an enormous yawn. Tears of boredom came into the girl's eyes, and she looked round to see if the men at the table near the stage had noticed. They paid her no attention. Any one of those men could be Paul, Sue thought, and that poor cow showing her tits could be me. Men aren't interested in sex any more; all they care about is money.

'Another bottle?'

Sue looked up to see who had spoken. She had long since ceased to notice the woman behind the bar, who was now flicking over the pages of a women's magazine. What's to notice? she asked herself, she's exactly what you'd expect behind the bar in a place like this, lavish, bleached blonde with a hairdo like shiny plastic packaging, a low-cut blouse showing the straps of the bra that achieved that unnatural cleavage, and a skirt where the length was probably half the circumference of the waist. She's just not young any more. So what?

'You look as though you could do with it,' the woman said. She pulled the cork on another bottle and sniffed the cork. 'Feel free,' she said, 'I'll join you. This one's on the house. You look like you've had the same sort of day I have.'

'Thanks,' Sue said, 'I don't mind if I do.'

If this bored barmaid's hiding a thwarted maternal instinct under that unlikely bosom, who am I to stop her? Sue thought.

They both drank in silence for a while, then Sue smiled and raised her glass. 'Men or money? Or rather, men and money, what's your excuse?'

'Is there ever anything else?' the woman said, lighting a cigarette. She offered the packet to Sue.

'I've given up twice,' Sue said. 'Here's to the third time.' She put the cigarette in her mouth and lighted it at a candle on the bar. 'My name's Sue,' she said, 'Sue Stockland.'

'I'm Vita.' The woman behind the bar held out her hand. Sue felt nails like cats' claws scratch her palm. 'This is my bar. I own it.'

'It's nice,' Sue said. 'The hall porter at my hotel said it was nice. It's quiet tonight, though, isn't it?'

'Monday's a bad night,' Vita said. 'Business only really builds up at the weekend, it gets really busy then.'

'Mondays are like that,' Sue said, and hearing the sound of her own voice, she knew she was getting drunk. 'I hate Mondays,' she said, 'but I guess so does everybody.'

That's not true, she thought, I love Mondays, that's the day Paul comes back to me from the weekends with his wife.

'I mustn't get drunk,' she said. 'I've got a lot to sort out in the morning. And then there's Paul.'

Vita was silent for a few minutes, then she sighed, resigning herself to listening to the story of Sue's life, and poured them both another drink. 'Who's Paul?' she asked.

'He's the man I love,' Sue said, 'and he loves me but he's got a bloody wife and two monster sons he can't leave so we can never be together except perhaps one day years ahead when I'll be too old for him to marry me.'

'But if he's not too old for you now, he won't be then,' Vita said.

But Sue was not to be consoled. 'Men don't get older like women do,' she said. 'It's not fair.'

'Oh, come on,' Vita said, 'it can't be as bad as all that. Look on the bright side. You probably have a better time with him than his wife does.'

'He hates his wife,' Sue said. 'I hate his wife. I don't know her but I hate her. She's dull and stupid and he only goes back to her at weekends because if he doesn't his monster sons break out and get into trouble. She can't control them. I think I hate his kids more than I hate his wife.'

'You should count your blessings they're not yours,' Vita said. 'I'd much rather be you than his wife. You can't really lose, can you?'

Sue wanted to say something serious to forward the discussion, but she found it hard to get the words she was looking for into some kind of order so she could speak them.

'What's he like?' Vita asked. 'Does he look like anyone? I go for the Russell Crowe type myself.'

'Paul's the most beautiful man I've ever seen,' Sue said.

'Ah, there you are, you see. All the women say that till they marry the prince, and then the scales fall from their eyes and they see him for what he is, not a prince but an ordinary old frog.'

Vita laughed and Sue started to get angry.

'Paul is beautiful,' she said. 'Look, I'll show you.'

She opened her wallet and took out a photograph of Paul. She pushed this across the bar to Vita. 'There,' she said, 'isn't he gorgeous? We were going out to a fancy dress party as Robin Hood and Maid Marian last New Year when it was taken.'

Vita glanced at the photo; then she started and picked it up to look more closely.

Sue took it back without noticing Vita's sudden interest. 'You see,' she said with a note of triumph, 'you think so too now, don't you? You thought I was making it up, how good-looking he is.'

'You're right,' Vita said, 'he's terrific looking. Wife or no wife, you're on to a winner there. What does he do?'

'Do?'

'For a living? Is he rich as well as gorgeous?'

'We never really talk about his work. He's in business.'

Sue found herself very tempted to tell this woman about how she wasn't at all clear about Paul's finances, how sometimes he seemed to be fabulously wealthy and then the next he was asking her to lend him money as though he was totally skint, but she suddenly saw that this was horribly disloyal. And as a businesswoman herself, she was well aware how the wealthiest entrepreneur could be personally strapped for cash in the short-term. She said, 'He's very rich, though. He drives a purple Lotus.'

'You don't say.'

Sue was beguiled by the apparent sincerity of Vita's interest. She found herself telling this unlikely confidante all about Paul. As she talked, it seemed to her that there was less to tell than she expected; she'd never thought about how little she really knew about him, but then she'd always wanted to keep his wife-life at a distance so she didn't ask. She didn't want to bore Vita, though, so she allowed herself to create a few details about

Paul's fabulous international connections and his houses abroad and the helicopter he was thinking of selling because it was difficult to land it in London now he'd moved his office out of a high-rise block with a landing pad on the roof into a whole house in the West End.

It was all lies, of course, but she had had too much to drink and she was enjoying herself making up stories. She felt much more cheerful now. But finally Vita began to stack glasses behind the bar. It was very late. The guitarist had stopped playing when the party of businessmen had left. Sue wondered what had happened to the pole dancer. If she depended on tips for her money, she must have had a poor night. Sue imagined her leaving without the price of a meal, walking into the city centre in the hopes of picking up a punter who'd take her to one of the sleazy hotels near the station for the night. Sue felt her eyes fill with tears once again as she imagined the plight of the dark-haired girl she had scarcely noticed, still wearing the red and black basque and the fishnets under the thin coat she clutched close against the cold. Well, there was no harm in making up stories about people; it probably made them more interesting than they really were.

I'm drunk, she told herself.

Vita clearly wanted to close the club and go home. She turned off the lights over the stage.

Sue got unsteadily to her feet.

'I've got to go,' she said, 'I've got to ring Paul. He must be home by now.'

'Will you be all right?' Vita asked. 'Do you want me to call a taxi?'

'No, I'm fine,' Sue said. 'The one good thing about having feet as big as mine, you don't topple over so easily.'

I can't believe I said that, Sue thought, I must be really drunk to joke about that.

Vita came round to the front of the bar to see her to the door.

The cold air in the street hit her and she had to lean against the wall to catch her breath.

'You sure you don't want me to call a cab?' Vita said.

'The air will do me good,' Sue said. 'I'm fine now. Thank you for the drink, and for listening.'

She started to walk away, then turned back to Vita.

'You saved my life tonight, letting me go on like I did,' she said. 'I really needed someone to talk to. I'm sorry I put you through it. Here's my card. If you're ever at a loose end in London, look me up. I'd like to buy you a drink.'

'Sure,' Vita said, 'I might just take you up on that.'

8 The Mark

No one took much notice of the man in a donkey jacket and jeans standing outside the Charing Cross Road entrance to Tottenham Court Road tube station, but the newspaper-seller on the corner was momentarily curious because he appeared to be lost and yet he was obviously not a tourist.

Then the man turned round and the newspaper-seller saw the glittering-eyed dragon tattoo on the back of the man's neck and he understood. The man must be a sailor, those tattoos were his personal souvenirs of ports the world over. But here he was like a fish out of water.

'Aw right, mate?' the newspaper-seller said.

The tattooed man stared at him as though he were speaking a foreign language.

'You talkin' to me?' he asked.

There was something about the dragon man's eyes which made the newspaper-vendor step back.

'Not me, mate,' he said, and hurried over to sell a paper to a woman in a taxi stopped at the lights.

The tattooed man crossed the road and walked a short distance along the north side of Oxford Street, then retraced his steps and turned left up Tottenham Court Road. Then he came back to the newspaper-seller.

'You know a sandwich bar up one of these streets?' he demanded.

The newspaper-vendor was used to tough customers, and he

knew how to look after himself; but there was something about this man which made him feel threatened.

'There's sandwich bars on all these streets,' he said. 'What's special about the one you want?'

'Search me,' said the tattooed man, and turned to cross the road again to the tube entrance on the west side of Charing Cross Road.

He looked to his right to make sure there was no traffic turning left out of New Oxford Street towards Cambridge Circus.

Then he stopped in his tracks. The man he was looking for was at that moment coming out of the entrance to the tube station entrance opposite.

The tattooed man had no doubts that he had found his mark. The man swaggering up Tottenham Court Road was the man in the photograph Saul had shown him. There was no mistaking him; he looked like a stage actor in a historical drama with those fantastic clothes and the sports shades in spite of the cloudy day.

The tattooed man plunged into the stream of traffic after his quarry, narrowly avoiding a motorcyclist who swore at him. He ignored that, also a woman who gave him a V-sign, and a van driver who had to jam on his brakes so suddenly that the car behind rammed the back of his vehicle. The tattooed man didn't even notice, he was so intent on keeping in sight the wide-brimmed black velour hat that his mark wore.

The tattooed man watched the man disappear into a scrum of people waiting for the lights to change. He thought he'd lost him, then saw that the man hadn't crossed the road, but was walking briskly towards Great Russell Street. He followed on the opposite side of the road until his quarry suddenly turned into a small side street and disappeared through a door in the wall.

There was a sandwich bar on the corner, with an entrance on to the main street. The door in the wall must lead to stairs to the floors above. Two floors, the tattooed man noted. A light came on in the top window above the bar. The mark couldn't be very fit, he'd taken a long time to get up the stairs.

There were two bells beside the door in the alley. The tattooed man could not make out the name on the top bell; the other was blank.

It took him only seconds to open the lock on the door and go into the building. It was too dark to make out anything but the uncarpeted stairs facing him. The only light came from a small window on the landing at the top of the first flight. From there, what illumination there was came from a skylight in the roof.

The tattooed man tried the door facing him at the top of the stairs. It was not locked. He opened it and walked into a room furnished with a metal table and a typist's chair. There was a pile of telephone directories on the floor, and a few box files on a shelf opposite the window.

The man he was after was sitting at the table and had picked up the telephone receiver and started to dial when his visitor entered. He had taken off the fancy hat and in the shabby surroundings of this room he had lost the theatrical bravura which had given his pursuer an extra thrill of anticipation over reducing the vain little shite to a pulp.

When the mark saw the tattooed man, he put the phone down.

'Who are you?' he asked, and his voice wavered.

The tattooed man knew at once that the pretty boy knew why he was there, even if he didn't know who he was. He threw a photograph on the table.

'That you?'

The mark shrugged.

The tattooed man picked up the photo and looked at it again. He clicked his tongue like a mother admonishing a child.

'The picture don't do you justice,' he said.

Then he flexed his fingers and added, 'On the other 'and, by the time I leaves yer, yer could say it's proper flattering.'

The mark said nothing. The tattooed man leaned across the

table and shoved his face forward into the other's until the two were almost touching. He smiled, showing his toothless gums in a grotesque parody of a threatening snarl which was the more menacing for its absurdity.

'Big Saul wants his money,' he said. 'All his money.'

The telephone started to ring. Both men stared at it until the answering machine clicked in and the ringing stopped.

The mark said, 'It's in hand. It'll take a few more days.'

'Saul says he can't wait no longer.'

The incongruous sound of the Crazy Dog ring tone suddenly blared from the mark's pocket. The man looked at his tattooed visitor, who shook his head.

The mark took out the mobile phone, turned it off without looking at it, and put it on the table. He started to plead with the tattooed man.

'Another twenty-four hours, that's all I need. I was let down. I'd have had some of it yesterday only something went wrong. I'll have it by the morning, and the rest next week, I swear I will. A friend who's selling her house has done an unofficial deal with a speculator through an agent and they've promised the money at the end of next week.'

'That's not the way Saul wants it, though, ain't that so? 'E said you didn't understand 'ow urgent is 'is need. 'E warned you, right?'

'Look, come back tomorrow and I swear I'll be able to give you something to tide you over. I'm getting the money from someone who'll have it for me tonight. Stall Saul 'til tomorrow and take my car now as a deposit, it must be worth something, it's a Lotus.'

'Saul don't drive.'

'You tell Saul you couldn't get hold of me today and you can have the car for yourself. I swear I'll have the money for you tomorrow. Twelve hours isn't going to make that much difference, surely?'

The tattooed man watched him. He was losing patience with this creep. The snivelling little sucker was sweating; he was grey with fear. The tattooed man could see him trembling. He wished that once, just once, one of these poncy little creeps would make a show of standing up to him.

But then, of course, he couldn't exercise the exquisite skills of his craft. It demanded real artistry to pulp a pretty face till it would be a long time before any girl worth trying it on with would look at him. And this time he was like James Bond in the movies; Big Saul had given him a licence to kill which was a lot more than just ruining some pretty boy's looks.

He was beginning to enjoy himself. He took off his donkey jacket with a flourish that a stripper removing her bra would have envied, and the rays of an orange rising sun on his chest dazzled the mark's eyes so that he looked away.

'You got a kettle in this dump?' the tattooed man asked. 'I could do with a nice cuppa tea before we get down to the business in 'and.'

9 A Midnight Caller

Lucy brought coffee into the drawing-room and turned to her guests.

'Who'd like a liqueur?' she asked. 'Or at least, there's Courvoisier, so the choice is, do you or don't you want that?'

'What's going on, Lucy?' Maxine asked.

'Yes,' Tara Burns said, 'you've been queer all evening.'

Quentin Burns said, 'She's right, actually, you have been sort of different tonight, Lucy. Is something up?'

Lucy felt suddenly overwhelmed by the scale of what she had done. Until that moment, she had been looking forward to the amazement when she told her friends. And they would be amazed: Lucy was the last person anyone would anticipate doing something so unexpected. Everyone in the village looked on her as their personal part of the bedrock of the community, immutable.

The excitement she had been feeling at the prospect of the unknown future had evaporated. Fear had been part of that excitement, and now, looking round at the faces of her good friends, only fear remained. Lucy wished she hadn't asked the Burnses and Max to hear her news. She made foolish, helpless gestures with her hands, unable to find words.

Maxine tried to help her out. She said, 'To what do we owe this sudden bout of generosity? Not that anyone could call you mean, of course, but this dinner in the middle of the week and then Courvoisier and a fire in the drawing-room – well, it's not your everyday event, is it?'

Lucy poured the Courvoisier and handed the filled glasses to her friends. Not only was this evening out of the ordinary, she didn't think they had ever had a meal together here except in the kitchen where the Aga kept the cold at bay. Certainly, she'd hardly ever lighted the fire in the huge open grate in the drawing-room before, not even when her father was alive. It had been a relief when the disused chimney didn't smoke, which she'd been afraid it would.

She looked round at her friends, at their expectant, questioning faces. She tried to smile and felt her dry lips crack with the effort.

'Tonight is special,' she said. 'I've got news.'

She wasn't sure where to start, explaining to them what she'd done. She wished now she hadn't kept Paul such a secret. When he came to stay the weekend, she never went out with him into the village. He hadn't wanted to and nor did she. For the very few hours they spent together, they wanted to be alone. And her house was quite isolated on the outskirts of the village. She'd never have kept her secret if she lived in the centre of the community. Only Maxine knew Paul existed and that was because Lucy had run out of excuses for refusing Max's invitations for Friday nights. Until Lucy and Paul fell in love, she and Max had gone to the pub together or cooked each other a meal on Fridays.

'Well, don't keep us on tenterhooks, is it good news or bad news?' Tara asked. She and Quentin exchanged looks.

Lucy glanced at Maxine and she knew that her friend thought she was going to announce her engagement to Paul. Lucy saw that Max looked apprehensive, not happy for her.

'Actually, I don't know for sure,' Lucy said. 'I don't know what I feel.'

'For God's sake,' Quentin said, 'shall we all come back same time tomorrow and maybe you'll be ready to tell us your awful secret by then?' He threw himself back on the chaise longue, which was much harder than he'd expected.

'Well, Lucy, what is it?' Maxine asked. She looked worried.

'I got you all here to say goodbye,' Lucy said. 'I've made a decision.'

She looked round at their faces. They all looked stunned.

'Goodbye? What do you mean, goodbye?' Quentin said.

'What part of goodbye don't you understand?' Tara asked him. She was attacking her husband because she didn't know what to say to Lucy.

'I've sold the house,' Lucy said. 'I'm moving on.'

'What do you mean, you've sold the house? Who'd buy this place, for God's sake. You can't have sold it.'

Tara got up and filled her glass from the Courvoisier bottle. Then she filled Maxine's glass, then Quentin's.

'What about me?' Lucy said. 'I'm in shock myself.'

Quentin took the bottle from Tara and filled Lucy's glass.

'What about your job with me?' he said. 'Aren't you going to work for me any more.'

'I'm sorry, Quentin, but I couldn't tell you. I didn't know myself till yesterday. The whole thing happened since the weekend.'

'The weekend?' Maxine said. Lucy couldn't meet her eyes. Please, she thought, don't mention Paul.

'Has this got anything to do with the love you dare not show in the village?' Maxine sounded as though she was not going to let this drop.

'A lover? You never said anything to me about a lover, Maxine,' Tara shrieked, 'are you running off with him, Lucy?'

'Stop it,' Lucy said, 'I've sold the house that's all, to a speculator who put the money upfront for a quick sale. I'm not running off with my lover. But it's time I brought about a few changes in my life.'

'What are you going to do with the money?' Quentin asked.

'She's not going to invest in your business, I can tell you that for nothing,' Tara said.

Lucy was shaking. God, she thought, I never thought it would be like this. I feel like a traitor to my own life.

And then she asked herself, How can I answer their questions when I know if I tell them the truth they'll think I've gone mad?

'This is about this bloke of yours, isn't it?' Maxine said. 'Paul's why you're doing this. Oh, Lucy, don't do anything without thinking it through.'

Lucy shook her head. 'Paul has a little girl who's got some terrible genetic disease,' she said. 'There's only one place in the world they have a technique which could possibly save her life, in America. It's going to cost a fortune, but it's her only hope. I'm giving her the money.'

'You're selling your home for that? Just like that?' Max couldn't even try to hide her shock. 'Who says they can cure this child? What's wrong with her, what's its name? Have you checked? No, tell me this isn't true.'

'Who is this fellow Paul?' Quentin asked. 'This is the first we've heard of him. What do you really know about him? Have you met this daughter of his?'

'Oh Lucy,' Tara wailed, 'it's a wonderful thing to do, but Max is right, do be careful.'

'He sounds like a right conman to me,' Quentin said. 'And what are you going to do for money? Afterwards. Where are you going to live?'

'Oh, stop it, all of you,' Lucy said. She hadn't expected her friends to like her plans, but she had thought they would at least make a show of being supportive.

'Why does it all have to be so final?' Maxine asked. 'Why do you have to go at all? Think about this. All right, you've done some deal and sold the house, but you don't have to throw everything away.' After a moment she added, 'You could live with me....'

'... And I'm sure I could manage another day's work each week if money's that tight,' Quentin said.

'Oh, Lucy, how can you abandon us like this. Nothing will be the same without you,' Tara said.

Lucy jumped to her feet and faced them. She could hear her voice break because she was very close to tears, but she took a deep breath and spoke out:

'You're all very good to me and the last thing I want is to lose good friends like you. But I won't, will I? We'll still be friends whatever happens. There's nothing I'd like more than to stay on here and pretend that nothing's changed. But you must see, I'm over thirty; I want to do a bit more with my life before it's too late. I want to try something else. No, Max, I didn't really think through what selling the house means, and I'm scared to death about what's going to happen, but what really shocked me was that once I'd done it, I felt really relieved and excited. I'm looking forward to a new life, really looking forward to it. Oh, please, try to be happy for me.'

They sat in silence. No one knew what to say. A log rolled forward in the grate with a flurry of sparks.

And then the telephone started to ring.

'Who's ringing you at this hour?' Tara said. 'It's nearly midnight.'

Lucy picked up the receiver.

'Yes?' she said.

The person on the line hesitated, then a woman's voice said, 'Is Paul Meyer there?'

'Who is this?' Lucy asked.

'I want to speak to Paul.'

'He's not here,' Lucy said. She didn't like the way this woman spoke to her, she sounded arrogant and peremptory. 'What's this about?'

The woman didn't answer at once. Lucy felt herself go cold. This must be Paul's wife, she told herself, he's told her about me and now she's calling up to cause trouble.

Lucy hadn't considered it before, but if she was going to pay for Julie to go to America for treatment, Paul would probably have to tell his wife how he'd got the money. She might be calling up to thank me, Lucy thought, but then she told herself, no, he'll lie about where it came from, he'll invent some benevolent donor or a charity or something to provide.

Lucy could hear the woman on the line breathing very quickly. She sounded upset. Perhaps she wasn't being peremptory, perhaps she was as disconcerted by Lucy as Lucy was by her.

It is his wife, Lucy told herself, it must be.

'Is everything all right?' Maxine asked in an urgent whisper. Tara and Quentin were watching Lucy curiously, not sure what to make of what they were hearing.

'My name is Lucy Drake,' she said slowly and clearly, as though her caller might not speak English. 'I can give him a message, if you like. What's your name?'

'I'm Sue, Sue Stockland.' The woman's voice sounded flat now, and dispirited. 'Are you expecting him tonight?' she asked.

Lucy blurted out, 'Are you his wife?'

How funny, she thought, I've no idea what Paul's wife's name is. I know about Julie, but he's never mentioned his wife except calling her Julie's mother.

There was a pause. Then Sue said, 'Paul and I live together. We're not married. So who are you, if you're not his wife?'

Lucy gasped. Maxine jumped to her feet and went to take Lucy's arm, but she pushed her away.

'What's going on?' Tara said, 'who is it?'

'Look,' Lucy said firmly into the telephone, 'whoever you are, if this is some sort of wind up, it's not very funny. Paul and I are in love, and we're planning to get married as soon as Julie's cured.'

'Julie, who's Julie?'

Lucy felt very relieved. This crazy woman, Sue or whatever she said her name was, couldn't know Paul very well if she'd never heard of his daughter.

'Julie's his little girl,' she said. 'She's very sick, so you see if you're some bimbo who thinks you're in with a chance of making it with Paul, you should think again. It's really not appropriate.'

Sue made an exclamation of irritation. 'Listen, you sanctimonious cow,' she said, 'Paul doesn't have a little girl. He has two brat sons who are supposed to be infant prodigies of some sort and they take every penny he's got. I should know, I've been providing most of the pennies. They're the bane of my life.'

Lucy couldn't take in what Sue was saying. She gestured to Quentin to pour her another Courvoisier and drank it in a single gulp.

'It must be a different Paul,' she said. 'There's been a stupid mix-up. My Paul definitely has a little girl who's desperately ill. I've sold my ancestral home to pay for her to go to America for treatment.'

Lucy deliberately used 'ancestral home' like that to bring a bit of light relief into the situation.

They were both silent for a moment trying to take this in.

Then Sue said, 'Someone's having us both on. I've put my business in hock to raise the money to pay for some tuition or equipment his bloody gifted children need to stay grounded on Planet Earth. Their mother is some drudge who can't control them. That's why he has to go home every weekend to bring a restraining influence to bear.'

'He's here every weekend,' Lucy said, 'he's at home all week to be there for Julie because his wife can't cope.'

There was silence while they both took this in. Then Sue said, 'What a bastard,' and there was a note of something like awe in her voice.

Lucy said, 'What's happening? Have you any idea what's going on? Why did you ring here? How'd you get this number.'

'A woman rang me and said she was his wife and she had to talk to him, it was urgent. She told me to dial 1471 on his private telephone at my flat and call the number to give him the message because that's where he'd be. It was your number.'

'Well if I'm his girlfriend and so are you, was she his real wife, do you think? Has she found out about us?'

'Or is she in it with him?' Sue said. 'I don't know how she got my number or knew about the telephone in my flat otherwise.' She hesitated, then went on, 'I can't believe he's such a bastard,' she said.

'My God,' Lucy said, 'how could anyone do that? I loved him, and I thought he loved me. I worried about Julie as though she was my kid, his and mine.'

'Ditto here about his sons. I even read books on child psychology and dysfunctional families to try to understand those thug boys of his,' Sue said. 'Believe me, I know how you're feeling. Have you given him the money?'

'No, but I've sold my house. I was going to give him the cheque on Friday.'

Oh, my God, Lucy thought, perhaps there's some mistake he can explain.

Sue said, 'And me, I've been taken for a sucker too. I've got a load of cash here waiting for him, £20,000, in notes in a brown envelope. I'd have handed it over already if he'd got home here tonight.'

Lucy said, 'I'm sorry, I can't talk about this any more. I've got to think. And where's Paul? Why isn't he here? Or with you, if he's not with his wife? Does he know she's blown his cover? I don't know what to do. What are you going to do?'

'Plan painful ways to kill him,' Sue said. 'As long as I keep hating him, I won't have to face how much I love him.'

'I could kill him, too,' Lucy said. She was aware that Maxine, Tara and Quentin were all staring at her in amazement. 'I never thought I'd say that about anyone, but it's true.'

She put down the phone and turned to face her friends.

'Don't ask,' she said. 'I don't want to talk about it to anyone, ever. You can see yourselves out. I've got to go to London, there's something I have to do.'

10 An Old Acquaintance

Detective Chief Inspector Guy Dugdale was bored, and that made him irritable. He hadn't joined the Met to investigate yet another anonymous corpse found dead of a heroin overdose among the rubbish bins in a puke-streaked alley in Central London. He was a highly trained detective and this case wasn't worthy of the money spent on his specialized training.

But a death was a death was a death, and he and Derek Malone had been the only detectives available on duty when the call came. Some snot-nosed little uniformed constable thought it might be a suspicious death.

'Get that constable's name,' Guy Dugdale said to Malone. 'I want to fix it so he's on the beat till his feet rot.'

Malone gave no sign of being impressed by his boss's urgency. 'Not such a good idea, sir,' he said, 'not as long as he's in our area if he calls for CID every time he stumbles over a dead druggie.'

'Then I'll get him transferred,' Inspector Dugdale bawled. 'Get me the right form and I'll sign it now.'

'I'll check on his name when we get back from checking this body of his,' Malone said calmly.

'OK, OK, have it your own way,' Dugdale said in a resigned voice.

'Some poor mother's son,' Malone said. He was unimpressed by Dugdale's hot air. Fundamentally Malone knew, and so did Dugdale, that they brought the best out in each other; they were a good team.

It was just beginning to get light, and the street sweepers were out in Piccadilly Circus and on Shaftesbury Avenue.

'Where is this place we're looking for?' Dugdale asked.

'It's off Frith Street,' Malone said, turning left and slowing down as they crossed Old Compton Street. 'It's up here on the left, I think.'

'Leave the car,' Dugdale said. 'This street will be jammed solid with delivery vans in the next hour, we'll never get away.'

They walked up the street past closed bars and restaurants and turned into the alley where a uniformed policeman stood waiting for them.

Before they got within earshot of the uniformed man, Dugdale said to Malone, 'Do you know, I had my first sexual encounter with a tom against the wall in this alley. This, or one exactly like it.'

'I don't suppose the lady would recognize you now, if that's what's worrying you, sir,' Malone said. 'It must've been a few years ago.'

'It was my Dad paid for it. Said it was time I learned the ropes from a pro.'

Malone clearly did not believe him. Dugdale wondered if his sergeant, a married man with four kids, had ever been with a prostitute.

'Well, if you're stuck for what to give your eldest on his thirteenth birthday …,' Dugdale said.

'This is it,' Malone said.

The body lay across a pile of rubbish bags: a white male, probably in his late thirties, fair-haired and wearing a suit. In his right hand, the fingers clutched an empty syringe.

'Oh Christ,' Malone said, 'here we go again. Another middle-class thrill-seeker who bit off more than he could chew on a night out in Soho?' Malone was glad he wasn't the one who was going to have to break the news to a wide-eyed little wife on some executive housing estate in Essex. He said, 'You couldn't get a much clearer cause of death, could you? What d'you think he did? Worked in a building society, or a jeweller's? Could've been a teacher, I suppose, frustrated that the kids in his class thought he was past it.'

'God knows,' Dugdale said. He turned to the uniformed constable. 'Any money on him? He wasn't short of cash, by the look of him. What wouldn't you give for shoes like that?'

The constable shook his head. 'Nothing on him, sir,' he said. 'No wallet, no car keys, no mobile telephone.'

'Some down-and-out probably found him before we did and took the lot,' Malone said. 'Whether this is an accidental over-dose or suicide, he did himself in.'

But Dugdale, giving the body a cursory glance, suddenly leaned forward and peered more closely into the dead face.

'No,' he said slowly, 'he didn't do anything of the sort. I know who the bugger is – or was, I should say. That flat-footed constable may be more right than he guessed when he called this a suspicious death.'

'Really?' Malone said. 'Because he's someone you know?'

'No,' Guy Dugdale said, 'because of the sort of people this joker knew when he was alive.'

Malone tried to look expectant, as if Dugdale were going to perform a card trick and he thought he should seem impressed.

But Dugdale didn't sound as though he was in the mood to draw rabbits out of hats. He sounded serious.

'His name was Paul Meyer,' he said. With one finger he shifted the face of the corpse slightly, then stepped back and turned away. 'At one time,' he said, 'Paul Meyer's was a name to reckon with in the Manchester underworld.'

'Are you saying you don't think this is some amateur over-dose?' Malone looked incredulous. 'The man's got his fist actually clamped round the empty syringe. What more evidence do you want?'

'Just so. That's what they want us to think. It's too good to be true. This is some of Paul's old pals getting their own back, and making it look like a self-inflicted accident. I don't suppose we'll even find any marks of violence worth talking about on the body, but I'd bet my pension he's been done over.'

'But why now? From what you say, they've waited a long time for their revenge. I'll check records, but I'm pretty sure he hasn't come to our notice down here.'

Malone wrote something in his notebook, then put it in his pocket.

Dugdale was impatient.

'Perhaps they took so long because they had to walk from Manchester on the legs this joker broke for them,' he said impatiently, 'how the hell would I know? Or care. This is a professional hit, so it comes to the same thing in the end. This fucker's not worth wasting more resources on finding who killed him.'

'If you're right, he's a murder victim. We've got to look into it,' Malone protested.

'Go through the motions if you have to. You won't get anywhere. Not in finding who killed him, or climbing the promotion ladder. It's up to you. I'll see you back at base later.'

Dugdale turned his back on Malone and walked away. He wanted to be alone for a while, trying to recreate in his head the sleazy and violent setting of Manchester's criminal world ten years or so before.

It was a painful process, made more difficult because he had worked very hard since then on trying to erase his own experiences in the city from his mind. His time in Manchester had been an unhappy period for him personally. Most of his colleagues had been tough, experienced local men who had worked their way up from the bottom. They automatically resented the new breed of graduate intake, and they particularly disliked Dugdale who had joined the force as a graduate lawyer who had been fast-tracked from the start by a chief constable who was still –

just – his father-in-law. Then, even after Connie divorced him, he never became one of the boys. He scarcely drank, he didn't know what the others were talking about most of the time because he didn't watch television or support a football team, and, as a rugby union player of at least some local note, he couldn't even pretend to see the charm of rugby league. Nor was he part of the thriving club scene where most of his younger colleagues were very much at home. And to top it all he wasn't a mason.

That was the world in which Paul Meyer appeared as Young Pretender to the godfather on the Manchester crime scene. God knows where Big Saul had found Paul, but he'd picked him out as a favourite son from the start. Meyer was young, very good-looking, very charming. He was everything that his mentor was not and he became the acceptable face of some very nasty goings on. Best of all, from the point of view of Meyer's boss, he had the advantage, as the protégé of an arch criminal, that he was ruthless, violent, viciously greedy, and entirely without conscience.

Dugdale wracked his brains, trying to remember what had happened. He himself had been moving on, promoted to the Met as a Detective Chief Inspector. His colleagues, who had long looked forward to his going, ostracized him as soon as he was appointed to London because they took this as proof that he thought himself too good for them. If he was honest, he'd probably lost touch with the Manchester scene some time before he actually departed.

But he hadn't failed to notice that by then Paul Meyer was no longer a major player in the criminal world there. Dugdale had been aware of that, but he hadn't asked questions. For one thing, he knew he wouldn't get answers; for another, he didn't think he would ever again have to care.

But as he pounded the Soho pavement aimlessly, trying to remember, he thought, I did have a theory, though, I remember that—

Dugdale passed the entrance to a strip club where the neon sign, showing a high-kicking naked female silhouette, was on the blink, the light flicking on and off.

His memory was suddenly triggered. He recalled a neon sign like that in a Manchester side-street, the figure of a Spanish bull-fighter in some sort of big hat. He'd seen Paul Meyer in the club there. Meyer had married one of the strippers. That's when he disappeared from the criminal mainstream. Big Saul never forgave him.

At least, that was my theory, Dugdale told himself. Big Saul was a romantic homosexual and he was in love with Meyer. And Meyer was ambitious enough to string his boss along except in the end when he'd done a stupid thing and blown his chances for ever by getting married.

Meyer was an arrogant little prick, Dugdale thought, he probably believed he was big enough by then to kick Big Saul in the teeth. But he wasn't. Big Saul was like a hideous octopus hiding in the dark shadows, his tentacles reaching into every sleazy cranny in the city's underworld. It would take a lot more than a vain and vicious wannabe to dent Big Saul's iron grip on his dominion of crime.

That's why Meyer came to London, Dugdale told himself, it must've been to escape from Big Saul. Except no one escaped from Big Saul and lived to tell the tale.

Dugdale stopped walking and looked around to orientate himself. He was under Holborn Viaduct. It wasn't an area he knew well. He stopped a cab. He had to get back to the office. He had a starting point now.

First he must find Paul Meyer's wife.

He found Malone in the canteen, snatching a quick breakfast. He'd thought he was safe for half an hour. Dugdale saw his sergeant's face change as he saw him coming, and for a moment he was grateful that Malone's complete imperturbability had so far stopped him taking a swing at his superior. Dugdale knew that his own obsessiveness was irritating. He wished he had waited for Malone in the office, rather than rushing to get him moving on what had to be done.

'Finish your breakfast,' he said, and noted the surprise Malone couldn't quite hide.

'You all right, sir?' Malone asked.

'Yes,' Dugdale said. 'Hang on, I'll get a coffee and tell you what I want you to do.'

'No, sir, I've finished. I'll make coffee in the office. You wouldn't want to drink the stuff they serve here.'

'You sure? You must be bloody hungry to eat in this place.'

'Needs must when the Dugdale drives,' Malone muttered, but under his breath. Dugdale did not ask him to repeat it.

Back at his desk, he told Malone what he remembered about Paul Meyer.

'I want you to find out about the wife,' he said.

'Presumably she won't be walking around calling herself Mrs Meyer?' Malone said.

'No, and I can't remember what she was called when she was working. One of those first names strippers call themselves. The Manchester lads might be able to help. Some of them must be old enough to remember.'

'Wasn't that your old force, sir? Do you want to call in outstanding favours yourself?'

Malone was teasing his boss. He knew what Dugdale's former Manchester colleagues thought of him. But though he could understand their feelings about his boss, he didn't have much rapport with those Northern proles either.

'No, no,' Dugdale said, 'you're good at getting people to do you favours. You go ahead.' Irony was not in Dugdale's intellectual repertoire.

'You only think that because you're not,' Malone said, again under his breath. He made comments like these to let off steam; it was what made it possible for him to get along with his boss.

Dugdale ignored him. 'I've got a feeling she'd got some sort of name from Latin, like a flower,' he was saying. 'Or perhaps it's legal, like *habeas corpus*. Something like that.'

'Narcissus?' Malone asked, being facetious.

'No,' Dugdale said, taking him seriously, 'that's from Greek.'

'Oh,' Malone said. 'Well, I'll get on to our plain-English-speaking Northern colleagues then, and see whether they remember a stripper with a handle like *habeas corpus*. It's not a name that's easy to forget, I'd have thought.'

'It was definitely a name with a Latin connection,' Dugdale said. 'That's what made me remember. She was a classic whore, anyway.'

Half an hour later, Malone came back to Dugdale.

'I've found Paul Meyer's widow,' he said. He did not try to pretend that he didn't feel pleased with himself.

Dugdale looked at him. 'Well?' he said.

'She's not called after a plant,' Malone said, 'perhaps you were thinking of Aloe Vera. Her name's Vita.'

'Well, there you are then, that's Latin. Vita, of course. Vita Virgo. I remember a story about her putting a man in hospital when he asked if he could get his money back under the Trades Descriptions Act. What's she up to these days?'

'I'm about to tell you that,' Malone said. 'An old friend of yours, a sergeant with a name that sounded like Windbreaker, said he thought she'd turned legit and given up the dancing and turning tricks. She owns a club in Manchester city centre called the *Fedora*. There's a small dance floor and live music and a few showgirls. She runs it herself.'

'I'll tell you something for nothing,' said Dugdale with a grin that told Malone he had given his boss exactly what he wanted, 'if Vita Virgo really went legit, she'll be up to her ears in debt by now.'

11 Motive and Opportunity

A t four-thirty in the morning all the birds in Regent's Park woke up and began to sing their hearts out. Why? Sue asked herself. What have they got to sing about?

It seemed extraordinary to Sue to hear that chorus of birdsong in the middle of a huge conurbation like Greater London. How could there be enough birds to make themselves heard above the constant rumble of traffic on the Marylebone Road?

She gave up pretending that she was even trying to get to sleep. All she could think about was the empty space beside her in the bed and the phone that didn't ring.

Time crept by. She tried to watch television, but in her bruised mind it was as though everyone was talking in foreign languages. She turned on the radio, but she felt as though she were eavesdropping on the electronic intimacies of robots. It was useless to try to distract herself from thinking about Paul.

And then Sue found herself thinking about Lucy Drake. It was hours since she'd made the phone call which blew the world apart for both of them. She wondered what Lucy Drake was doing at this moment. Had she sat in the dark all night thinking about Paul? Was she listening to bloody birds shouting their heads off outside her bedroom window? Sue asked herself, Is she thinking about me? Is she crying her eyes out because now she knows that Paul loves someone else? Lucy Drake didn't sound like the kind of woman who took a man being unfaithful in her stride; she was probably thinking the world had come to an end. And it has, Sue thought, for her and for me, it feels like there's nothing left.

She saw Lucy Drake as a faithful little creature who would be shocked rigid by Paul's betrayal. And Sue seemed to remember her saying something about flogging the ancestral pile to pay for treatment for Paul's fictional kid. She almost felt sorry for her rival.

Sue wanted to mock Lucy's naïveté, and then she thought, I'm not so different. I don't know how to bear Paul betraying me. A country bumpkin wife was one thing, but a full-blown mistress is something else entirely. I can't bear it. And he's taken me for a ride over money, too.

So she rang Neville. It seemed an age before he answered the phone, and when he did he sounded as though he had a heavy cold.

'You sound awful,' Sue said, 'don't tell me you're back on the drugs?'

'Not the way you mean, I'm not, but I took a pill to get to sleep and then I've no sooner got off when you wake me up. I feel like death.'

'Please Neville, you've got to come. I really need you.'

'Do you know what time it is?'

Sue tried to ignore the real anger in his voice.

'I know,' she said, 'I'm sorry, but I wouldn't ask if I weren't desperate.'

'What's happened?' Neville sounded resigned, still thick-headed.

'Paul hasn't come home.'

'He often doesn't.'

'No, you don't understand. Something's happened, he's been lying to me.'

'He often does.'

Sue was irritated. Neville wasn't taking her seriously.

She said, 'He got me to raise some money for him – and if you say "he often does" I'll kill you. This time it was a lot of money.'

There was a short silence, then Neville said, 'I don't see there's anything you can do except wait till he turns up. You can't go out searching for him.'

'I've done that,' Sue said, and her voice sounded flat and hopeless. 'I went out searching all the pubs and clubs he might be in, but there's no sign of him. I rang the hospitals, too, but no one knew anything about him. Should I ring the police, do you think?'

'Not yet. They won't take any notice.' Neville seemed to think he might sound unsympathetic, so he added, 'He hasn't been missing long enough. He has to be gone a certain number of hours before they take any notice. They'll think he's picked up another woman somewhere. Which he probably did.'

Sue hesitated. 'He's got a girlfriend in Devon,' she said. 'I found that out tonight. He spends the weekends with her. But he's not there. I tried that.'

'Go to bed with a stiff whisky and if he hasn't turned up by morning, then ring the cops,' Neville said. 'I'll see you tomorrow.'

Sue listened to the dialling tone for some time before she put the phone down herself.

She filled the kettle to make yet another cup of coffee. She wanted a brandy, but something told her that she should stay sober.

She sat and watched an interminable old film about star-crossed lovers simmering in the jungle. She made up her mind that at eight o'clock she would take some sort of action. That was the earliest time you could stretch to call normal working hours. There was no point in ringing round before that.

The more she tortured herself about Paul, the easier it was to dismiss Lucy Drake as any kind of real threat. It just wasn't possible that he'd ever loved Lucy Drake. The woman must have set out to seduce him. He must've been drunk. She sounded like the type who'd read more than intended into a lighthearted seduction and take a kiss as a proposal of marriage. But he'd known Lucy Drake well enough to press the right buttons to get money out of her. Lucy obviously didn't know Paul any better than Sue knew him herself.

On the stroke of eight, suddenly determined, she picked up the phone and dialled directory inquiries for the number of the police. She asked them to put her through.

She tried to explain to the sleepy-sounding cop on the switch-board that she was probably over-reacting, that she hadn't seen Paul since yesterday morning, and that it was unusual for him not to ring if he was delayed at work.

'What does he do?' the policeman asked. 'What does he do for a living?'

It was a routine question and when she said she wasn't sure exactly, she sounded ridiculous. 'He's in business,' she said.

'What sort of business?' the policeman asked.

'Something to do with clubs, I think,' she said.

'What kind of clubs is that, madam?' the policeman asked. 'Gentlemen's clubs, special interest clubs, sports clubs, night clubs…?'

She was afraid the cop was going to ask if she even knew what Paul looked like, but he didn't. He took all sorts of details from her, then said he had to check.

There was a long delay then before she heard the policeman's voice come back on the line.

'We'll be in touch at once if we have any news,' he said, rather hastily, she thought. 'Let me confirm your address and tele-phone number?'

He read the details back to her, then said something non-committal and the line went dead.

He thinks I'm wasting his time, Sue told herself, he was going through the motions but he's got me down as a hysterical bitch who's driven her boyfriend into doing a runner. He fobbed me off. She took up the mug of cold coffee and drank it.

She jumped as the doorbell rang. Her heart began to thump and she found it hard to breathe.

Two policewomen, one in plain clothes, the other in uniform, stood outside.

'How did you get up here?' Sue asked. 'Why didn't the doorman ring me from downstairs?' That bloody Ted, she thought, he'll have to go.

'We didn't see anyone,' the plainclothes officer said, holding up an ID card.

Sue felt the conversation was getting surreal.

'What do you want?' she asked coldly.

'Are you Sue Stockland?'

Sue's first reaction was to make some smart-ass comment about police who rang innocent people's doorbells at dawn asking stupid questions like that, but she didn't. She already felt that she was trying to put off an evil moment.

'You rang the station asking about Paul Meyer?'

Sue nodded. Her insides felt as though they had turned to water.

'Does Paul Meyer live here?'

Sue nodded. She turned and the plainclothes policewoman followed her into the sitting-room.

'What's happened? Is Paul in some sort of trouble?'

'May I sit down?'

Sue was irritated by the woman's attitude. Why couldn't she come out with whatever she had to say? She sat down opposite the policewoman. The girl in uniform waited in the hallway.

'I'm afraid there's been an accident,' the policewoman said.

She's good, Sue thought, she's obviously doing this all the time, she doesn't give a damn, but she makes it sound as if she cares.

'Is he hurt? What's happened. Just tell me?'

'I'm very sorry. Paul's dead.'

'You're lying to me,' Sue said, 'this can't be true.' And she thought, How dare she call him Paul?

The uniformed officer suddenly appeared with a glass of water.

Sue raised her arm to push the girl away, but her hand caught the glass and the water splashed into her own face.

'I'm sorry,' she said, wiping her face on her sleeve. 'I know you're only doing your job. Tell me again, did you say Paul is dead?'

'We need a formal identification, but I'm afraid there's not really any doubt.'

'What happened? Was he in a fight? Where is he?'

'Was he a regular drug user? We think the cause of death may have been an overdose of heroin.'

'Paul? A drug user? Are you crazy? He hated drugs, he was a respectable business man, the father of two gifted sons.' Except he wasn't, Sue thought. She'd forgotten that he wasn't.

'That bitch killed him, that little country mouse,' Sue said suddenly. 'She did it.'

There was a short silence. Then Sue asked, 'What happened? Where did this happen?'

'His body was found in the street in Soho,' the policewoman said. 'Who did you mean when you said "she killed him"? Who do you think might have killed him?'

'Her name's Lucy Drake and she lives in the country, some-where in Devon. I don't know exactly where, but I've got her telephone number. She was Paul's mistress.'

'One of his mistresses, do you mean? You were his mistress too, weren't you?'

Sue nodded. Then she said, 'We only found out about each other last night ...' she hesitated, trying to keep track of time, '... yes, last night.'

'So did you quarrel with Mr Meyer about that?'

'I've told the police, I haven't seen him since early yesterday.'

The policewoman leaned forwards towards Sue. 'Sue,' she said in her tone of phoney familiarity, 'if what you say about the time of your call is right, Lucy wouldn't have had time to get from the country to kill him in Soho, would she?'

'You could've got the time of death wrong,' Sue said, but she knew she didn't sound convincing.

'We think he may have taken the overdose voluntarily,' the policewoman said.

'I suppose I'll have to ring Lucy and tell her.'

'If you give us her address, we can do that. We'll send someone round.'

'I told you, I don't know her address. Why do you ask questions when you don't listen to the answers? You can have her telephone number, but I'll ring her anyway.'

'It's up to you,' the policewoman said. 'As far as we're concerned at the moment, she's not part of our inquiries.'

'Do you want me to identify him?'

The plainclothes policewoman gave Sue a hard look, then turned away.

'No, that won't be necessary. We will need to ask you some more questions as the investigation goes ahead, but that can wait. We're trying to get hold of his wife, she's next of kin. You knew he had a wife, of course?'

'Yes,' Sue said.

'We'll get his wife to identify him,' the policewoman said.

The two of them left at last. They tried to be kind, asked if there was anyone they could call to keep her company.

Once the policewomen had gone, Sue sat down and tried to think of something appropriate to do.

It's like watching something really good on television, she said to herself, and there's a power cut and everything goes blank. Then she thought: Lucy Drake will probably feel the same when she knows he's dead, she must have thought she loved him, too, in her own way. That's enough motive to kill him.

Sue tried to imagine Lucy Drake, an overweight girl with braids, wearing a baggy tweed skirt and shapeless sweater, sitting in front of an open fire with her apple cheeks streaked with tears. She, too, would be wondering about the wife, the woman who had made the mysterious phone call that had led Sue to telephone her, the woman who was neither the mother of a handicapped daughter nor of brilliant sons.

But there was a wife. The police had given Sue the impression that Paul hadn't been in touch with her, though she couldn't be sure why she'd thought so. It was bad enough discovering there was another woman, but a real-life wife he hid away behind all those lies of his, that made the feeling of being betrayed much worse.

Does that mean she inherits? Sue asked herself. Paul appeared to be a rich man, even if he had personal cash flow problems sometimes; he'd mentioned property he owned in the country, an old manor house in Devon, which must be how he met Lucy. And his business seemed to be successful. If he'd made a will, it wasn't likely he'd leave everything to a wife he hadn't seen for years, but on the other hand, Paul was a youngish man, it probably never occurred to him to make a will at all. Why should it? He was full of life and he wasn't the type to plan for the future.

It's no good, I've got to call Lucy, Sue told herself. I can't help it, I want to talk to her, there's still something unresolved between us even though Paul's dead, we both shared him and thought he loved us and that connects us whether we like it or not. Lucy's probably the only other person in the world who can understand how angry I feel with him.

It's awful that that's all we have in common, Sue thought, we're worse than strangers, we're enemies.

Sue felt nervous as she dialled Lucy's number. She wasn't sure what she should say. As she listened to the ringing tone, she wondered how long it took those policewomen not to feel nervous when they told people about the deaths of their nearest and dearest.

Lucy answered the phone and suddenly sounded wary when Sue said who she was.

'I thought it might help us both to talk,' Sue said.

'What about?' Lucy said. 'I don't see that we've anything to say to each other. We'll both have to work things out with Paul, not each other. Have you seen him?'

Sue had never had to give anyone bad news before; or, at least, she'd fired a lot of people at work for all sorts of reasons, but this was different. Her relationship with Lucy, or rather her lack of one, made it difficult. Lucy was her enemy, and she was Lucy's. They had to hate each other because Paul had told each of them that he loved no one else but her, and they had both believed him.

'Haven't you heard about Paul?' she asked, her voice trembling.

'What about Paul?' Lucy said. 'I drove straight up to London last night after we talked. I meant to find him and have it out with him, but I couldn't get any reply from his office and he wasn't at any of the places he's mentioned in the past, so I came back here and he hadn't even left a message. If he's with you, you're welcome to him. As far as I'm concerned Paul Meyer is history.'

Oh, no, you're not getting away with it as easily as that, Sue thought, you can't just opt out.

Sue felt she needed to be brutal.

'He is history now,' she said. 'He's been murdered.'

She put the phone down.

She sat for some time staring at nothing. She was remembering what that plainclothes policewoman had said, that Lucy couldn't have killed Paul because she wasn't in London. And she kept hearing Lucy's cold, bland voice repeating, 'As far as I'm concerned, Paul Meyer is history'.

'She wanted him dead, she could have killed him,' Sue said aloud. 'She had a motive for wanting him dead, and she could have killed him.'

12 The Voice of an Angel

A phone was ringing in the main CID office. There was no one in the deserted room to answer it.

Detective Chief Inspector Dugdale, who was looking for Malone, tried to ignore it, but it was against his nature.

When he did answer it, there was something about the voice of the woman on the other end of the line which caught Dugdale's attention. Instead of fobbing her off when she asked to speak to someone to give information about a murder, or simply telling her to ring back later and talk to the duty sergeant, he told her to hang on while he put the call through to his own office.

Once seated at his own desk, he picked up the call and said, 'Now, tell me what this is about?'

'I know you're going to think I'm off my head,' the caller said. He wanted to say he didn't care, he just wanted to hear her talk. He loved the sound of her voice; it was husky and seductive and what his grandmother would have called musical. Thinking of his grandmother didn't seem inappropriate: the caller didn't sound old, far from it, but she sounded old-fashioned. He could listen to her all day.

'Of course I don't,' he reassured her. 'We solve a lot of our crimes because people like you help us with information.'

'My name is Lucy Drake,' she said. 'I'm calling you from Devon.'

Dugdale was disappointed. 'I'm afraid we don't cover Devon

from here, Miss Drake,' he said. 'It's not like Scotland Yard in Sherlock Holmes's day.'

Lucy laughed. 'Oh, I know that. The murder I'm calling about happened in London.'

Suddenly the life had gone out of that bewitching voice and Dugdale was afraid she was going to cry. 'It's about the death of Paul Meyer,' she said, and her voice caught as she said the name.

Dugdale was intrigued. He couldn't imagine any connection between Paul Meyer and a woman in Devon with a clotted cream voice, but he was eager for her to tell him anything she wanted. He wanted to go on listening to this girl for as long as he could.

'I think I know who killed him,' Lucy said. She sounded a little breathless, as though she couldn't herself quite believe what she was saying. 'I'm sure he was killed by a woman who called herself his girlfriend. Her name is Sue Stockland and this is her telephone number.'

She started to recite the number, but Dugdale interrupted her.

'Can we get a few things clear before we get down to details,' he said, sounding like a kind old uncle. 'What exactly is your connection to Paul Meyer? And why do you say he was murdered? I have to tell you we're still investigating the cause of his death, and we definitely haven't ruled out that it could have been an accident or suicide.'

'Paul would never commit suicide. We loved each other too much,' Lucy said.

Oh dear, Dugdale thought. He was disappointed. 'An accident, then?' he said.

'Well, I suppose it's possible it was manslaughter rather than murder, but however Paul died, I'm sure Sue Stockland caused his death. She threatened to. On the telephone, she said she was going to plan painful ways to kill him.'

'Have you any real evidence to back up this very serious accusation you're making?'

'She was the one who told me Paul had been murdered. She said murdered. If even the police haven't decided it was murder, how was she so sure, unless she killed him? It's your job to get the evidence. I've given you the information on Paul's killer, and it's up to you to prove she did it. Isn't that how it works?'

Dugdale was at a loss as to what to say. It's just my luck, he thought, I talk to a girl who sounds like an angel, and before I can even find out if she looks as good as she sounds, she turns out to be certifiably crazy.

To Lucy he said, 'You could help by answering a few questions if you wouldn't mind. Like how well you knew Paul Meyer? I don't mean as lovers, which I assume you were, but did he ever talk to you about his business, for instance? Or his wife?'

Lucy did not answer at once. She felt a strong urge to talk to this man who sounded as though he cared about her as well as about who killed Paul. She wanted to tell him about Julie and how she'd made herself homeless to raise the money to give to Julie. But none of it's true, she told herself; Julie wasn't real, Paul made her up. I've got to get that through my head, none of it's true.

'I can't talk about this over the telephone,' she said.

'I could send someone down to interview you at home there in … where is it, Devon?' Dugdale said. 'I could say you're a material witness.'

'No,' Lucy said firmly. 'I wouldn't want to talk to just anyone. I'm coming to London tomorrow. It's a long story, but I've sold my house and made myself homeless so I'm going to stay with my friend Helen in Canonbury for a week or so while I decide what to do.'

'Can you come to my office? We could talk quietly here, off the record.'

'No,' Lucy said. 'All this is very personal and private and I won't be able to tell you properly in a formal office. Can I meet you for lunch? You must take time out for lunch.'

'I'll tell you what,' Dugdale said, 'I could take you out for dinner tomorrow night. Then we could have a really informal, unofficial personal chat about all this. If we can use anything you tell me as part of the official hunt for Paul's killer, and you agree to this, then you can make a formal statement at another time.'

Dugdale was glad that Malone wasn't listening to this. He knew exactly the way the sergeant's raised eyebrow would be showing his disapproval. Official police procedure in a murder case didn't include dinner dates with suspects. Dugdale had read the file. He knew that Sue Stockdale, another of Paul Meyer's girlfriends, had accused Lucy Drake of murdering him.

Lucy was hesitating. Dugdale was surprised at how much he wanted her to say yes.

'OK,' she said. 'I'd like that. And then I can tell you off the record why I'm sure Sue Stockland is the person you're looking for, without you having to arrest me for defamation of character or whatever the crime is. I loved Paul and I know I'm right.'

`

13 The Gorgeous Policeman

'Oh, Neville, I'd no idea I could miss anyone so much,' Sue said.

She was lying on the sofa in the sitting-room of her flat with her feet tucked under a cushion to hide them from her own eyes. Such big feet, she felt, made a mockery of the tragedy she was suffering. She wore no make-up, her hair was unwashed and she was wearing a baggy old tracksuit which, she could see from the pained expression on Neville's face, her high-camp friend would be ashamed to give to a charity shop.

Neville was looking at her with concerned distaste. 'But, darling,' he said, 'this is so not you.' He was embarrassed for his friend that she had let herself go like this.

Sue turned her head into the back of the sofa and started to cry again.

'Look at me,' she wailed, 'I've nothing left to live for.'

'I know, my pet,' he said. 'Nothing whatsoever.'

'This is no time for your kind of humour,' she said.

'I'd have thought it was just exactly the time,' he said.

'If Paul could see me now, it would break his heart. Look at the state I'm in.'

'I'd really rather not,' Neville said, but under his breath. He didn't know how to cope with a woman in this condition. It was always so much easier dealing with emotional wallowing in other men. Women were so *gross*, they took themselves so seriously, they were such drama queens.

Sue howled: 'I can't sleep, I can't eat, everything reminds me of Paul. We were so happy and now I can't see any point in going on without him because he'll never be coming home.'

'Oh, darling girl, don't you think we're being the teensiest bit *excessive*? You'd scarcely been with Paul for two years, and no doubt he was perfection, but he wasn't always the centre of your world, was he? And from what you say, you certainly weren't the only love in his life.'

'Yes, yes, but I never looked at another man.'

'Darling, you will some day. Probably soon, the show must go on. How can you conceive of depriving the world of the wonderful, brilliant, life-enhancing woman that was Sue Stockland long before she met Paul?'

'My life only started when he came into it....'

'I know, darling, how I know! But that's our secret. The *hoi polloi* must never know that. You are a star. You have a public, you have clients, dependants, the world of public relations looks to keep the wheels of commerce turning. All over London people are depending on Sue Stockland for their employment, their livelihoods, their families' future....'

Sue rolled over to face him. She was trying not to laugh even as she still wept.

'Stop it, Neville, you're a monster. It's true, it's horrible without Paul. I never realized how much I'd miss him.'

'Well, darling, how could you, after all? You'll get over it. It's not as if you've never been in love before, is it? You've loved and left enough of them in your time, now you're getting a taste of your own medicine. Call it emotional homeopathy.'

'Don't be absurd, I didn't *die* on them.'

'They probably wished you had,' Neville said, not quite under his breath, but not quite loud enough for Sue to be sure what he'd said.

'I never really loved anyone but Paul,' she said again, her face showing renewed signs of crumbling.

'Now don't go into another of your little pets,' Neville said.

He looked at her, then, in a voice that didn't sound like his at all, he added, 'I'm not surprised you feel suicidal if you've glanced in the mirror and seen what you look like. For God's sake, woman, have a bit of pride.'

Sue, surprised at his brutal tone, recognized that he really meant what he said. She swung her feet to the floor and stood up. 'Is it that bad?' she asked.

'It's enough to turn milk sour,' Neville said. 'I didn't go through the horrors of the damned in rehab to have to sit and look at a wallowing woman. Come on, you are what you look like, remember. Repair the ravages, we're going out.'

'I can't Neville, I feel terrible.'

'I won't take no for an answer. Get some slap on and we'll go on the town. While I'm waiting, I'll work out an itinerary of bars with low lights. I've got my reputation to think of, too.'

Sue laughed. The doorbell rang.

She looked shocked, then frightened. 'God,' she said, 'for a moment I forgot, I thought it must be Paul. Who else can it be, I don't know anyone?'

Neville put his hand on her arm. 'It'll pass, that not believing he's gone,' he said.

Sue was grateful to him for trying to comfort her.

'I know,' she said. 'I know, I'll get used to it.'

She went to open the door. 'That bloody Ted,' she said, 'he's supposed to ring up and warn me if anyone comes.'

She knew at once that the two men in plain clothes standing in the corridor were police. Is it their big feet? she thought, looking down at their shoes.

'Who are you?' she asked, aggressive because they had inadvertently made her think of her one absurd weakness.

'Detective Chief Inspector Dugdale and Detective Sergeant Malone,' Malone said, showing her his identity card.

Sue thought of asking Dugdale for his, but something about

him stopped her. She gestured them to come in. She glanced at Neville, wondering whether to introduce him. He was looking at Dugdale open-mouthed. Sue wondered why, and gave her visitor another look. What she saw startled her. He's gorgeous, she thought, he's the best-looking policeman I've ever seen. Maybe the best-looking man.'

'I'm Neville,' Neville was saying, taking Dugdale's hand and shaking it. 'I'm a friend of Sue's, here to offer succour in her hour of need.'

He's twittering, Sue told herself, what's the matter with him?

Dugdale ignored him; only Malone nodded to acknowledge him.

'I presume this call is in the line of duty?' Sue spoke in her most business-like tone and thought, What do I look like? The best-looking cop in London comes to see me and I look like nothing on earth.

'You lived here with Paul Meyer, I believe?' Dugdale asked.

'I think I'd better go, darling,' Neville said, 'this is obviously official business, I should let the dog see the rabbit. Call me later.'

As soon as Neville had closed the door behind him, Sue said, 'You'd better sit down.'

She went to the sofa and sat with her back to the light. Dugdale sat in the armchair facing her, and Malone, rather than sit beside her on the sofa, remained standing.

'Yes, Paul and I lived here together for two years,' she said to Dugdale.

'When was the last time you saw him?'

'He got up and went out to work early on the morning he died. I was half asleep, but I remember him going out.'

'What did he take with him?'

'What do you mean, what did he take with him? Wallet, car keys, stuff for work? The same as anyone going to work.'

'No suitcases, then?'

Sue wondered what he was getting at. 'Not that I know of,' she said. 'Perhaps he'd got a bag packed and picked it up on his way out, how should I know?'

Malone smiled at her and said, 'We are only trying to establish exactly what he did and where he went that day. He might have been going away on business for a day or two – that kind of thing.'

Sue shrugged and shook her head. 'Not that I know of,' she said.

'Would you say you and Paul Meyer had an open relationship, Ms Stockland? You don't seem to have taken much interest in what he was doing.'

'We weren't married,' she said.

'No,' Dugdale said. He smiled at her and she wanted to burst into tears so that he would put his arms round her to comfort her.

He said, 'I'm dying for something hot to drink, and I'll bet you could do with something yourself. Would you mind if Sergeant Malone goes into your kitchen and makes us coffee?'

Without waiting for Sue to say yes or no, Malone turned and started to leave the room.

'It's the second door on the left,' Sue said lamely.

'I'll find it,' Malone said over his shoulder.

Dugdale leaned forward towards her. 'Do you know a woman called Lucy Drake?' he asked.

Sue hesitated, frowning a little as she considered what to say.

'I know who she is,' she said. 'We talked on the telephone the night Paul … didn't come home. She told me she was a friend of Paul's.'

'Yes,' said Dugdale, 'yes, she was.'

Sue seemed to make up her mind. 'OK, if I tell you something, it's strictly between the two of us, right?'

'Of course,' Dugdale said. 'You can tell me anything you like.'

Sue looked into his eyes, brown long-lashed eyes which

seemed to mesmerize her. My God, she thought, tearing her gaze away, he must lead his wife a hell of a dance. If he's still married, that is, he looks like he's not much of a one for long-term commitment.

She sat back on the sofa, afraid that if she didn't draw away, she wouldn't be able to stop herself kissing him.

'I told this to the woman officer who came to tell me Paul had been killed,' she said, in as non-committal a voice as she could manage. 'I don't think she took me seriously. And then I thought I was jumping to conclusions because I was jealous. But I'm sure I'm not.'

'What did you tell her?' Dugdale asked gently.

'Lucy Drake killed Paul,' Sue said.

Dugdale said nothing.

'I told that woman, but she said Lucy couldn't have killed him because she was in Devon when Paul's wife told me to ring her and give Paul a message. I thought that was true, so I tried to put it out of my mind. But Lucy Drake was in London, she came to London after my phone call, I know she did because she told me. She was so upset that night she left directly after my call and drove to London to look for Paul. At that time of night it wouldn't take much more than three hours. She could easily have been in London when Paul was killed.'

'I'll check on that,' Dugdale said. 'She may've been clocked speeding if she managed that time.' He smiled at Sue. 'But tell me about the call you got from Paul's wife. What did she say exactly?'

'She said she was his wife and she had to get in touch with Paul urgently.'

'Did you know he had a wife?'

'Yes, he'd told me he was married. But the woman who said she was his wife on the telephone wasn't what I expected. She didn't sound at all what I'd imagined.'

'What exactly do you mean by that? What did you expect?'

'Oh,' said Sue, 'someone like Lucy Drake seems to be. You know, rather simple, a bit of a sucker, a kind of bumpkin. The wife I talked to on the phone wasn't like that.'

'What did you think she was like, then?'

Sue paused, going back over the phone call in her head. 'You know,' she said at last, 'there was nothing soft or put-upon about her. I think she had a Northern accent. And she sounded familiar, like someone I know.'

'Who? Do you know who?'

'No, it's just an impression. It's no one I know well. I think it must've been a politician I've heard on television. Or an actress, perhaps, an actress or a news-reader. It's funny how you get familiar with people's voices and think you know them, isn't it?'

Malone came in then with the coffee on a tray.

Dugdale got up to go. 'There's no time for that now, Sergeant,' he said.

Malone put down the tray on a sideboard.

'Do you have to go?' Sue said to Dugdale.

Malone smiled at her.

'Sorry,' Dugdale said, 'there's no time to spare, we've a murderer to catch. Enjoy your coffee.'

She saw the two men to the door.

Dugdale let Malone go out first, then turned back to Sue.

'Here's my card,' he said. 'It's got my mobile number on it. Ring any time, if there's anything you think I should know. That includes any unexpected visitors trying to get access to this flat. Or calls from strangers asking for Paul or saying they were friends of his.'

Sue was alarmed at his tone. 'Do you think someone was after him?' she asked.

Dugdale shrugged. 'We can't afford to ignore any possibility,' he said. 'Not in his business, although it could be quite innocent. Maybe the woman who said she was his wife is still looking for him, who knows? But I'd like to know anyway.'

It was some time after Dugdale and Malone had left her that Sue remembered what the handsome Detective Inspector had said about the business Paul was in.

I wonder what kind of business that policeman thinks Paul was in? she thought. Respectable successful businessmen don't get into that kind of trouble. That cop made him sound like some kind of criminal.

14 Big Saul

In his cramped, over-heated office, four floors above an alley off Frith Street, Big Saul sat at a table and glared at the individual standing opposite him. This man wore a tight black suit and the dragon tattoo on the back of his neck bulged above the collar of his shirt, as though somnolent after a heavy feed.

'You've screwed up,' Saul said.

'It wasn't my fault,' the tattooed man said. He was nervous and he dabbed at his toothless mouth with a dirty wad of Kleenex after saying the 's'.

'You didn't do what I told you,' Saul said.

'I did, boss.' The tattooed man made a sucking sound so as not to spray Saul, then went on, 'You told me to get the money and then get rid of him.'

'But you didn't, did you. You haven't got the money.'

'That's only because someone else did 'im in before I could.'

Big Saul reached across the table and grabbed the tattooed man by the collar, twisting it tighter until the man's face began to turn purplish.

'You mean you didn't even kill him?'

The tattooed man did his best to shake his head. Saul let him go.

He gasped a few times to get his breath. 'I'm trying to tell you, boss, 'e was dead when I went to deal with 'im.'

Saul leaned back in his chair. 'Tell me what happened,' he said.

The man shuffled his feet.

'I found out where the geezer 'ad 'is office and I went up after 'im. Well, we 'ad a little chat an' 'e told me 'e'd 'ave the money in the morning, and seein' as I knew 'ow much you wanted the cash, I thought it best just to frighten 'im and then come back in the morning. An' when I did, the pavement outside 'is office was crawling wi' Old Bill an' they was takin' our friend away in a body bag.'

You didn't happen to overhear what happened to him, did you?'

'Overdose, I think.'

'Did you rough him up? The police may think it was suicide if he's not marked up.'

'It could 'ave bin. 'E could 'ave topped 'imself. There weren't no marks on 'im, 'cos I'd got it in mind meself for 'im to meet with an un'appy accident. When I was in the Army we 'ad other ways and means of makin' sure we got what we wanted out of those as didn't co-operate.'

'I've got to get that money somehow,' Saul said. 'The bastard must have at least some of it hidden away. Perhaps it's in his office.'

'No,' said the tattooed man, 'first thing I did after I got there, I made him watch me search the place. They start to sweat if you get close, but this 'un didn't. I made him open the safe, too, but there was nothing there.'

'It must be somewhere. He'd be too scared not to have scraped some of it together.'

The tattooed man showed his gums in a grin. 'There you are, you see, it's the effect of the shock of the death of a geezer I was talkin' to only 'ours before he was promoted to glory. I was forgetting to tell you what I got out of 'im as a result of my skill in putting that psycho pressure on people like 'im.'

He paused to wipe his sleeve across his mouth.

Big Saul waited. 'Well?' he said at last.

'Well,' his employee said, 'let's say 'e didn't 'ave the money 'imself, not to 'and at least, but 'e told me where it was 'e was getting it.'

He stopped, wondering how he could make it clear to Big Saul that he deserved some sort of credit for saving Big Saul's bacon. But he couldn't think how to phrase this thought without causing offence.

'Well, spit it out, then.' Saul didn't try to hide his exasperation.

'Well, our friend was a bit of an 'it with the ladies, it seems. At the present time – at least before he was killed – 'e 'ad two of them on the go. Two very rich ladies. They've got the money in their 'ot little 'ands ready to 'and it over.'

'My God,' said Big Saul, 'that only gives us several hundred to choose from.'

The tattooed man looked hurt. 'You sells me short, boss,' he said. 'I made 'im tell me their names before I left 'im for the night. One of them lives in Devon.'

Saul looked at him with surprise and also with some reluctant admiration. 'You've done better than I expected,' he said. 'You screwed up, sure, but you did redeem yourself in the end. You know what to do now, don't you?'

'I'm on my way. One of the dames is 'ere in London, but the one as 'as raised most of the money, thousands and thousands she's got, that's the one as lives in Devon. I thought she should be the first.'

Big Saul thought about this. 'No, the London one will be easier to deal with. Get her money first, then you can take a little more time over the one in the sticks.'

'The only problem about that's I don't know where she lives in London,' the tattooed man said. He sounded sheepish, and stepped back as though expecting Big Saul to hit him. He added, ''E said as 'ow she was in Manchester, which was why 'e 'adn't got the money.'

'You know what to do?'

'Shouldn't be too difficult at that,' the tattooed man said, licking his wet lips. 'What's more natural for the grieving widder, in a manner of speaking, to chuck herself off a convenient railway bridge?'

'Having first made a donation of all her money to her lover's favourite charity....' Saul started to laugh at his own joke.

The tattooed man looked puzzled. 'What's that?' he asked, frowning.

'Me,' Big Saul said, and roared with laughter. The tattooed man joined in, and Saul suddenly stopped laughing and said, 'Do what you have to. And don't mess up this time. Get the money, shut her up for good and get out of there.'

'You can trust me for that,' the tattooed man said. 'I'll get a train to Devon and hire a car there. I quite fancy a few days in the country.'

'Do what you have to do, but don't you ever forget that any entertainment on the side you've got in mind for yourself before you knock them off, that's not what this is about. Getting my money comes first, and getting rid of the witnesses second, get it? Your kind of sex leaves marks and DNA and clues for the cops to trace so don't do it. Understood? Do this right and you'll earn enough to keep you in women for weeks.'

'OK, OK, you don't 'ave to tell me 'ow to do my job,' the tattooed man said. 'I'll be in touch when I've got it done and dusted.'

15 Know your Enemy

Lucy couldn't believe what she was doing. She had picked up the telephone and rung Sue Stockland's number without thinking. Put the phone down, she told herself, don't do this, it's a bad, bad idea.

'Hallo?'

Lucy did not recognize Sue Stockland's voice. It sounded as though it might be her grandmother, rather weak and depressed. Lucy put the phone down. She felt relieved. For some reason it made her feel better that Sue Stockland had someone with her.

That was a lucky break, she thought. I must've been mad to do such a thing. What would I say to her anyway?

Her own telephone rang. She picked it up, expecting Max or Tara with yet another suggestion about what she should do next.

'What is it this time?' she said in mock exasperation.

'Lucy? Were you trying to talk to me? This is Sue Stockland.'

Lucy still didn't really recognize the voice as Sue Stockland's, but she knew that it was her. She sounded so frail, though.

'I did 1471 and called you back,' Sue said in her old woman's voice.

'I don't know why I rang,' Lucy said. 'I just found myself doing it.'

'I did it too, I rang you yesterday,' Sue said, 'but you must've been out. I didn't leave a message.'

There was a pause. Then Lucy said, 'What happens now?'

'I think they're looking for his wife.'

'Yes,' Lucy said. There was a longer pause.

Then Sue said in a tentative way, 'You weren't talking about the police, were you?'

'No, I suppose not,' Lucy said. 'I don't know what I meant. How do you feel?'

'Bad. You?'

'Very bad. I can't explain, it's like being lost in a foreign country where they're out to get you.'

'It's not like just breaking up with someone, or even someone dying. I feel that if I could only think it through properly I'd find an answer. But I don't even know the question.'

'I know,' Lucy said, 'even my friends seem like strangers.'

Sue was about to say she didn't have any friends but she realized just in time that what she saw as a sign of strength would make her sound pathetic to Lucy. Lucy wasn't the type to understand that even a woman should be independent.

'Bastard,' Sue said.

'What?'

'Paul,' Sue said, 'what a bastard. I can't believe what he did.'

Lucy hesitated, then, with a doubtful tone in her voice, she said, 'That's what really hurts, what he did. Worse than his being dead, even. I feel as though he's demolished everything I'd built up in my life. I don't even know who I am any more.'

'I can't even hate him,' Sue said. 'All I want is to have it out with him, but he's given me the slip.'

'I think that's why I rang,' Lucy said, 'because he did the same thing to you. No one else could possibly understand.'

'Yes,' Sue said. 'I suppose that helps.'

'Yes,' Lucy said, and she thought, it does help. If I don't know my friends any more, it helps to get to know my enemy. It's something to build on, anyway.

16 Looking for Vita

There were times when Guy Dugdale thought he would have liked to be one of the boys, out drinking in the pub all evening, every evening, talking about work and setting the world to rights. Or, at least, putting the worst villains behind notional bars. And, of course, Dugdale didn't play the computer games the young lads in uniform liked so much, where Robocop defeated the evil-doers at the zap of a mouse.

This was one of those times when Dugdale wished he had the gift of sociability, for the only resource he had after working hours was to sit alone at his desk and go over and over the case in his head. An exercise of brainpower which often stole him a march over his convivial colleagues.

But there were several reasons why he found it difficult to get to grips with the killing of Paul Meyer. For a start, he found it hard not to find himself fighting against ghosts from his own past which made him uneasy about delving too deeply into the Meyer case. If he was honest, it wasn't just that; it wasn't only the past that troubled him: he had suffered from being an outsider in Manchester, and, though he had grown a much thicker skin since then, he was afraid that he was still an outsider in London. And this time he wasn't the one who suffered, it was the efficiency of his team that bore the brunt of his character flaws.

Then there was a problem which he seemed to have created for himself without quite knowing how it had happened. He had got involved on a personal level because of the two women who had suddenly erupted into a simple murder case with their recriminations and accusations. Malone, or even a detective constable, should be dealing with them, but somehow the women themselves had made sure that that hadn't happened. And what made it worse was that he wasn't sure that one or other of them wasn't playing him for a fool. Dugdale knew only too well that most murder victims were killed by their nearest and dearest. Of course he would argue to Malone that his personal involvement was a ploy, simply the best way of investigating these two suspects, but Dugdale knew this wasn't really true. The fact of the matter was that he was sailing too close to the wind; he knew he had to watch his step with these two female suspects or he could be in trouble.

And the final reason he was finding it difficult to deal with Meyer's death was that all his instincts told him that the killing was a simple gangland execution, a professional hit. In which case, Dugdale believed that his investigation was a waste of time and resources.

Which, he told himself, was probably why he had allowed himself to get so personal about it. It was all right for him to waste his time for the sake of Lucy Drake's creamy country voice and the attentions of a seductive streetwise predator like Sue Stockland, but he could be abusing his juniors if he let them get too involved in a hiding to nothing.

It was nearly nine o'clock and Dugdale thought he was alone in the office. He heard hurrying feet in the corridor outside, and Malone suddenly opened the door and burst in.

'Good God,' Dugdale said, startled. 'The noise you made running up the passage, I thought at least it must be someone wearing seven league boots, or Sue Stockland!'

Malone laughed; he, too, had noticed the size of Sue Stockland's feet, and Dugdale suddenly felt a surge of something that was almost affection for him.

'What are you doing here at this hour, anyway, Sergeant?'

'I've got a breakthrough and I wanted to tell you before I went home.'

'Well, spill. What is it?' Dugdale gave no sign that he was impressed at Malone's dedication, but he was.

'I've found Paul Meyer's wife.'

'Have you now? And where is she?'

'That's the point, sir, really. Vita Meyer's in London, and has been since the day Meyer was killed.'

Dugdale looked intrigued. 'I know what you're thinking, Sergeant. You're thinking maybe that the motive behind this killing is some sort of love triangle.'

'I don't think geometry has a shape for the number of angles involved in Paul Meyer's love life,' Malone said. 'But yes, I'd add her to the list of suspects. At the top.'

'So would I, Derek, so would I. You've done well. Did one of my erstwhile Manchester colleagues come up trumps?'

'No, sir, they didn't seem to be interested, beyond mentioning that she owns a more or less legitimate club in the city centre.'

Dugdale shrugged. 'I don't suppose it helped the cause to mention my name. Sorry.'

'Actually, sir, it was their attitude which started me probing this. They pissed me off, the way they messed me about. So I rang Vita's club and said I was her uncle and asked for her and they told me she had left suddenly and was in London. It turned out she went the morning before Meyer was killed. And then I tried the places in London where we know Meyer spent time, and one of the girls at the *Hell Hole* said a woman who said she was his wife had gone there looking for him that evening.'

Malone sounded breathless when he'd finished speaking.

'Now that's interesting, isn't it?' Dugdale said.

He had clearly launched himself on a new line of inquiry, and Malone had no intention of interrupting his train of thought. He nodded but said nothing.

Dugdale said, 'Why would a woman go out of her way to tell one of the girls at Paul Meyer's watering hole that she was his wife? And this is a woman who, as far as we know, hadn't had anything to do with her husband in ten years, a gal who always used her professional name when she was with him, and who had never been seen before round his London stamping ground? I presume she hadn't, anyway?'

Malone thought that his boss was thinking aloud, but he suddenly found himself fixed in the glare of Dugdale's impenetrable eyes.

'Well,' Dugdale said, sounding impatient, 'what do you think?'

Malone was at a loss for an answer. He wasn't sure he understood the question.

'She might be trying to establish possession,' he said, waiting for a stream of scorn to be unleashed over him.

'I think we're on to something interesting here,' Dugdale said. 'She wanted to establish her rights of possession as a wife. She was looking for Meyer to remind him that she was his wife. Why? What did she suddenly think she was going to get out of that unless she expected him to die?'

Malone knew better than to interrupt.

Dugdale went on, thinking aloud, 'Of course she may have announced she was his wife because she was afraid that something might happen to her if she found him. In which case she was out to get something from him to buy her off, and was afraid he'd get rid of her if he could. But that's speculation. Get hold of some recent pictures of Vita, we'll see if anyone else remembers her. Do we know any more?'

'Yes, sir, we do. I hadn't thought it was relevant but it could be. My wife's family come from Manchester, sir. I made a few calls around. Vita may have gone legit, but she isn't making money. You were right, she's up to her ears in debt and her backers at the club are about to foreclose. She's bankrupt. That's the local gossip, anyway.'

Dugdale was about to say something when the phone rang. He picked up the receiver impatiently and barked into it.

'Dugdale. Who's this?'

Malone turned away discreetly as Dugdale's tone changed.

'Ms Stockland,' he said, 'Sue. What can I do for you?'

He bent his head down as if he was trying to hear a whispered confession.

'I can't tonight,' he said, 'I'm hours late for an appointment already. Maybe tomorrow? A drink after work? Fine. See you then.'

He put the phone down, looking embarrassed.

'That was Ms Stockland,' he said. 'You know, Paul Meyer lived with her before he got himself killed.'

'I know who Ms Stockland is,' Malone said wryly. 'Dark hair, 38 bust, long legs and big feet.'

'She wants to talk to me about Meyer.'

'That's romantic,' Malone said and knew his boss had heard because he went a bit red.

But Dugdale ignored the crack. He said:

'Good work tonight, Derek, I think we're getting somewhere at last. Tomorrow you can find where Vita's staying and we'll drop in for a chat. Now go home before Mrs Malone starts phoning the police to report you missing.'

'Oh, that's all right, this is one of her class nights. She says she's not going to wait at home for me to come back from work every night, so she's taken up adult education classes at the local college. She's a lot more use than she used to be; she's quite a good carpenter, and she's done some of the mechanical repairs on the car. I believe the next thing she'll be starting to learn is how to build brick walls, but there's not been any call for that yet.'

Dugdale was not sure how he should respond to this unexpected domestic insight. 'The next step will be to brick you in, I suppose,' he said.

Malone smiled, but Dugdale felt that the sergeant expected something more from him.

'I'd suggest a drink,' he said, 'but I've got a dinner date. I'm already late.' He realized that Malone might think that unlikely and believe he was making an excuse to avoid socializing with him, so he added, 'I'm meeting Paul Meyer's country girlfriend, the woman from Devon. She's got something to tell me, she says.'

'It's amazing that Paul Meyer should be such a fascinating topic of out-of-hours conversation, isn't it, sir?' Malone said with a knowing look. 'I hope you can lead them on to more interesting subjects to talk about.'

Dugdale caught his eye and they both laughed. 'I know, I know,' Dugdale said, 'but they're so sad, it would be rude to refuse. What is it about apparently normal women that invariably makes them choose the bastards who'll hurt them? Anyway, listening is the least I can do, I suppose, and you never know, they might have some useful information.'

'Yes, sir,' Malone said, 'they might at that.'

'I'll let them down lightly,' Dugdale said, more to himself than to Malone. 'I'll tell them I'm married.'

'That didn't seem to put them off Paul Meyer, did it, sir?' Malone said.

'I didn't mean that. I meant … no, I'm not sure what I meant exactly, but I've a feeling I'm going to need a strategic retreat.'

17 This Time It's Real Love

'I hope you don't mind my asking,' Tara said to Lucy, 'but we're your closest friends and we're all dying to know; how's it going with the mystery lover?'

Lucy winced. If only they didn't know that Paul had ever existed, she thought, I'd never have to tell them.

But they did know; she did have to tell them, she was staying with Tara and Quentin and she owed them that.

'He's dead,' she said.

'He's what?' Quentin said and then added, 'he can't be dead.'

'Do you mean you've broken with him so he's dead to you?'

Maxine spoke in that tone people use when they're talking to the disabled.

'He was murdered,' Lucy said.

She knew she could make things easier for herself by being more forthcoming to these close friends, but she found it physically difficult to say anything about what had happened. She didn't want to talk to them about Paul.

'He was what?' Quentin managed to say.

'Is that why you rushed off like you did the night we were here for your goodbye dinner?' Tara asked.

'No,' Lucy said, 'it hadn't happened then. The police say he was killed later that night.'

'You didn't see him in London, then?' Tara said. 'Presumably you went to look for him when you left us?'

Lucy hesitated. She didn't want to explain about Sue

Stockland and her telephone call that dreadful night. 'I thought he was in trouble,' Lucy said. 'But I couldn't find him.'

She knew how lame she sounded, but she couldn't bear the thought of having to give further explanations.

She saw Tara and Maxine exchange an odd look.

'What's the matter?' she asked.

And then she thought, God, they're thinking I might have killed him myself. And, of course, they'd heard her threaten to do just that in her conversation that night on the phone to Sue Stockland. Oh, she asked herself, why does this all have to get so complicated? What does any of it have to do with them?

Tara laughed, then looked horrified at herself.

'It's nerves,' she said, 'it makes me nervous to talk about people dying.'

Tara had been on edge all evening, Lucy thought. She wondered if her friend had quarrelled with Quentin again. Living in the same house, she was aware of the tension between them. She'd told herself that things might be easier as long as she was there, a third party in the house. Perhaps she was imagining things, but Max obviously felt something of the same embarrassment, she'd stopped dropping in so much. But Lucy told herself that having her in the house wasn't awkward like having a stranger there, she was more like a member of the family. In spite of being homeless, Lucy still thought of the village as home. She'd taken it for granted that Tara and Quentin Burns also thought of their home as a temporary extension of hers. But perhaps they didn't. Lucy's life might have fallen apart spectacularly, but nothing had really changed for anyone else in the village, not even for her closest friends. I should have known, Lucy told herself, that's the nature of village life.

Certainly, her return was not much like a real homecoming.

The speculators had already started to demolish the house that had been the family seat for more than two centuries. This hadn't come as a shock to her. She'd rung up the buyer after

Paul's death, hoping to cancel the sale by giving the money back, but it was too late. She had been warned there was no going back, there was nothing she could do about it now.

But she wanted to hang on to the comforting feeling she'd once had of belonging here, and she thought she could best do that by refusing to acknowledge even to her friends what had really happened with Paul. She knew, of course, that they were bound to be curious about the bombshell she had dropped when they last had dinner together not much more than a week ago, in the half-derelict dining-hall in her old house.

So she'd decided that she had to tell them that Paul was dead. What she wanted to keep to herself was the extent of her own folly.

My life is still here, she said to herself, but it will have to be different.

She said aloud, 'It's incredible that the other day, the last time we were all together, I'd sold my house and I was going to leave the village and start a new life and I did it. But now, ten days later, I've done all that and I've come back because this feels like the right place for me to be.'

They all made sympathetic and supportive mutterings. Then Lucy dropped her bombshell. 'And, can you believe,' she said, 'I'm in love, really, really in love?'

'But I thought you were going away because you had been in love,' Quentin said, looking confused. 'And now he's dead.'

'Oh, God,' Maxine said. 'What have you done now?'

'I've met someone and I realize that I've never been in love before, not truly in love,' Lucy said. 'That's why I want to come home and settle down. Honestly, I never imagined that my life could come full circle like this in less than a fortnight and yet be utterly changed.'

'But you were settled down here when you fell in love before,' Quentin said. 'How can you call that progress?'

'He's married, isn't he?' Maxine said. 'Oh, God, not again.'

'Yes,' Lucy said. 'He's married. He told me that at the very start, but I don't care. This time it's different. With Guy, it's as though we're equals. This time I know I've got to stand on my own two feet, not expect him to take care of me. Any woman who marries a man as fantastically gorgeous as Guy must know someone else is going to grab him if she can. His wife must have got used to that by now.'

'Let's hope you are still saying the same thing when it's your turn to let him move on,' Tara said. So far that evening Tara had been quieter than usual and now when she spoke everyone fell silent.

'Have you slept with him?' Maxine asked at last and they all watched as Lucy's face illuminated with remembered pleasure. She simply couldn't hide her joy.

'Yes, she has,' said Tara who looked as though she might cry.

Lucy could feel her face going red with embarrassment. 'Is it that obvious?' she asked.

'Oh,' Tara said, giving Quentin a hard look, 'you get to know the signs.'

She went over to the Aga and refilled the cafétière. Quentin tried to catch her eye as she returned to the table to fill her guests' cups.

'I'll open another bottle,' he said, getting to his feet.

'Suffering from *déja vu*, my darling?' Tara asked and her voice was like tearing silk. 'But why not? There's not much that can't be put right by another bottle of vino, is there?'

Lucy was totally absorbed by her own feelings. 'But there's nothing to be put right for me,' she cried, 'that's what I want to tell you. Everything's worked out for the best. This time, with Guy, I feel I've been liberated and now I've sold that great derelict house and I've got a bit of money, everything's going to be perfect.'

Quentin opened a fresh bottle of wine and filled their glasses.

'If you're serious about coming back, there's a cottage for sale near the church which might suit you. It could have been designed as a love nest.' He smiled at Tara and she gave a little shrug.

'I know that cottage,' Lucy said, 'the estate agent told me about it.'

'And Quentin hasn't got anyone to replace you at work,' Tara said.

Quentin grinned at Lucy. 'God, please come back to work,' he said. 'It's been absolute hell trying to cope without you.'

'Who is he? This new married man?' Maxine asked suddenly. She sounded harsh, and her voice cut through the conversation. 'Who is this Mr Right who's apparently the one size fits all dream of womankind? Where does he come from? What does he do?'

Tara looked horrified. 'Oh, Lucy, don't tell me he's unemployed. He's after your money. He knows you've sold that benighted mansion of yours and he wants you to support him.'

'Do you think I'm an idiot?' Lucy said. She didn't see the look Tara exchanged with Maxine, a look which said that was exactly what they thought. 'He's a cop. He's a Detective Chief Inspector in the Metropolitan Police. So you don't have to worry about his being some sort of conman trying to swindle me out of my money, do you?'

Maxine ran her hands through her short hair so that it stood up all over her head.

'So that's all right, then, is it?' she said.

Lucy, quite unconscious of Max's intended sarcasm, smiled, grateful for her friend's apparent attempt at understanding. Then Max said, 'Do you mean to tell us that this man you've fallen for is the cop who's investigating the murder of the late Paul? Christ, Lucy, when are you going to have a bit of sense?'

No one said anything. The silence became oppressive.

'Lucy, do be careful,' Tara said suddenly. 'You can't know much about him, you've only just met. Quentin, tell her not to do anything irrevocable until she's sure.'

Quentin put his hand on Tara's shoulder. 'She's right,' he said to Lucy, 'one good shag doesn't make a summer, not to put too fine a point on it.'

'Listen to him, Lucy,' Tara said. 'He knows what he's talking about – for once.'

The two of them exchanged a smile and something raw and sexual in the way they looked at each other made Lucy wish that she was back at the old house on a Friday night waiting for Guy, not Paul, to arrive.

Maxine made no attempt to hide her contempt for Lucy's revelation. Clearly, she would have liked to give her friend a good shaking.

'You're making a complete fool of yourself,' she said, 'even more than the last time.' She sounded angry. 'Two weeks ago you were mooning around all week waiting for your one and only love to leave his wife in London and come down for a weekend of non-stop sex. Now suddenly all that's over and you're in love with another man. Talk about acting on the rebound.'

She leaned across the table and took the bottle of wine from Quentin to fill her glass. She drank it straight down. Her voice trembled as she said, 'I thought I knew you, Lucy, but at the moment I don't recognize you. What kind of woman are you?'

She banged the empty wine glass down on the table and said furiously, 'I could actually weep for you, you're such a fool.'

'Ease off, Maxine,' Quentin said, 'it is Lucy's life.'

Now's the moment to tell them how Paul made a complete fool of me, Lucy told herself. I should tell them how he was two-timing me, and how he conned me with the story of a sick daughter into selling the ancestral home and almost made off with the money.

But she couldn't do it. She couldn't tell them what kind of rat the man she'd thought would be the love of her life had turned out to be. They'll think that's what making me irrational, she thought. They'll make me out to be some sort of pathetic victim, but I'm not a victim. Whatever happens between Guy and me, I'll make my own decisions this time. Paul played my emotions like a fish on a hook; he nearly conned me out of everything I've got. And then she added, he did con me out of everything I've got. It was only because he was murdered that he failed to collect. Well, I'm not stupid, I've learned my lesson. At least I know I can trust Guy.

And then she thought, I wish I hadn't told them. But I had to tell someone. She surprised herself with the notion that if she told anyone, it should have been Sue Stockland.

Maxine was saying, 'And this policeman you're in love with is actually working on Paul's murder?'

'Yes, he is,' Lucy said, and she was surprised at her own defiant tone until she saw the look on Maxine's face and knew instinctively that her friend was thinking that Guy Dugdale might be baiting a trap for her because he suspected her of killing Paul.

He can't be doing that, Lucy told herself, that's crazy. Guy couldn't possibly do a thing like that.

But then she had a moment of doubt.

Could he? she asked herself. After all, I don't really know him at all.

18 A New Widow

Malone had discovered that Vita Meyer was staying at a small hotel close to Euston Station. She had booked in using her married name and she had opted to pay weekly rates.

'That's a good sign,' Dugdale said as he and Malone parked their car in a side street off Eversholt Street. 'She got off the train and went to the first hotel she came to.'

'Why's that a good sign exactly?' Malone said.

They started to walk up the street looking for Vita's hotel. Malone was irritated because he'd put all his change into the meter while Dugdale had put his hand in his pocket and come up empty. He felt like arguing.

Dugdale said, 'Don't you think it suggests she came on the spur of the moment? No premeditation. I spy a motive. Something forced her hand and, with a woman of Vita's sort, that means she suddenly discovered something to her advantage.'

'So you think something happened in Manchester to remind her that she was still married and she hot-footed it down here to see him?' Malone said. He was more irritated now because his boss was giving him nothing to argue with.

'Well, it's a possibility, isn't it?' Dugdale said.

'But why? After all this time, why should she think it worthwhile making contact with Meyer?' said Malone, who took it very much for granted that he was still in love with his own wife and she with him. He saw other people's relationships, too, in simple terms. 'She'd managed perfectly well without him for years,' he said.

'Except that she's facing bankruptcy, isn't that right? Money, Malone, money is the only conceivable reason for her coming.'

Malone thought of the corpse he'd seen lying sprawled on rubbish bags in a sordid alley off Frith Street. As far as he could recall, Paul Meyer's clothes were quite flash – fairly cheap but not much worn. His shoes were good, too. Malone remembered that Dugdale had made some remark to the constable on the scene comparing them favourably with police issue footwear. It hadn't occurred to Malone until this moment that Dugdale was suggesting to the constable that he swap with the corpse while no one was looking. Probably one of his weird jokes.

'Did Paul Meyer have money?' he asked.

Dugdale shrugged. 'Lucy Drake had raised several hundred thousand to give him,' he said. 'She told me that herself.'

'So your dinner with her paid off?' Malone said.

Dugdale looked embarrassed. 'Yes, yes, I'd say we both got something we wanted out of it. She needed someone to talk to, and I got some useful information.'

'That's all right then, sir,' Malone said and there was something in his tone of voice that made it sound mocking.

Dugdale heard it. 'What I'm trying to communicate to you, Sergeant,' he said, 'is that we don't know the state of Paul Meyer's finances yet. On the surface he seems to have been flush enough. That purple sports car, the flat that's all but Regent's Park, and, apparently, business interests in what for want of a better word we'll call the leisure industry.'

'And yet he'd asked Miss Drake for money. A lot of money.'

'And she was going to give it to him,' Dugdale said, 'and for all we know women all over London had been liquidizing their capital assets and giving him their money. He's maybe got a stash of millions hidden away somewhere.'

'He didn't have any money on him when he died.'

'After he was dead he didn't, you mean. Before he died he could've been walking about loaded. His killer could've got away with thousands. Or another passer-by, who saw his corpse before we did, could've nicked it.'

'Miss Stockland might be able to help us out here, about Meyer's money,' Malone said.

'I'm hoping so. I'm seeing her tonight to ask her that very question.'

When Malone heard this he almost laughed out loud. 'Did anyone ever warn you about the dangers of mixing business and pleasure?' he said, making no attempt for once to speak *sotto voce*.

Dugdale ignored him. 'Isn't this the hotel we're looking for?' he said. 'What a dump! Don't try to tell me again that Vita isn't desperate for money.'

The hotel was a standard early Victorian five-storey terraced house with a basement to which there was no access from the street. A printed sign hanging in the front window advertised vacancies.

'Pity the poor devils who come down to living permanently in a place like this,' Malone said.

He followed Dugdale into a narrow hallway with a small reception desk set into a space below the stairs. Dugdale seemed like a giant in this place, his broad rugby player's shoulders squeezed against the walls on either side of the hall as he walked ahead.

There was no one at the reception desk. Dugdale picked up the register and ran his finger down the page looking for Vita's name.

Malone was looking at a board with numbered hooks for room keys.

'How do they get that many rooms into a house this size?' he said.

'However over-crowded they are, they're better off here than on the street,' Dugdale said. 'We're not here to do Health and Safety's job. Vita's in Room Twelve, on the fourth floor, so you can do the sums for yourself later if you're interested.'

There was a tiny lift that had somehow been squeezed in the space alongside the stairs, but it wasn't working. They set out to walk up the stairs. Malone stomped after Dugdale's broad back, trying to keep up. He told himself, I'm glad I don't have to play rugby against him; getting tackled by him would be like being run over by a steamroller. Then he remembered that Dugdale had stopped playing for the Metropolitan Police first team because he thought he was too old. He's certainly fit enough still, Malone thought, and he can't be all that much more than thirty. He decided his boss must have some other reason for retiring and then he thought that, given the recent evidence of Dugdale's attractiveness to female witnesses, perhaps there was a woman behind his decision.

On the fourth-floor landing Dugdale turned back to watch Malone struggle up the last few stairs. Dugdale was not even breathing hard, but Malone was in a bad way.

'You're letting yourself go, Derek,' Dugdale said.

'I don't know why you gave up rugby,' Malone said, panting a little. 'Nobody could say you aren't still up to it.'

Dugdale grinned. 'Pure vanity,' he said. 'When I got promotion, I was told I'd have to do more interviews on television. I've been lucky so far, but no one wants to see a policeman who looks like a prizefighter on the screen.'

Malone wasn't impressed. Personally, he liked to feel that policemen should look as though they could defend the innocent public by putting the boot in against the criminal fraternity, rather than overgrown male models with lah-di-dah accents and a string of university degrees.

Still, when Vita Meyer answered Dugdale's knock at her door, Malone could see that his boss's appearance oiled their way into the room. Malone almost felt sorry for his boss if he had to take the attentions of women like Vita Meyer seriously. Malone was young, only twenty-five, so perhaps Vita was not as superannuated as she appeared to him, but she certainly looked over forty even in a dim light. She wore too much make-up to hide the lines round her eyes and mouth and her blonde hair looked crisp from over-bleaching. Malone thought she was repulsive.

When they introduced themselves she tried to get them to leave.

'I'll meet you later in the lounge,' she said. She had an accent Malone thought might be Liverpool. 'There is a lounge down there somewhere,' she said. 'It's the room where they serve breakfast.'

'Don't waste my time, Vita. If you won't talk here, we'll make this formal and do it at the station,' Dugdale said.

'What's that with the Vita?' she said. 'It's Mrs Meyer to the likes of you.'

'We're here about the murder of your husband, Paul Meyer,' Dugdale said.

Vita stared at him. Dugdale's expression did not change. Perhaps Vita took this as cruelty, or a lack of sympathy for her loss. She sprang at him like a cat, snarling, tearing at him with her nails.

Malone moved forward to restrain her, but Dugdale hooked a finger under her chin and held her at arm's length. He laughed.

'May I say how sorry we are for your loss?' he said, pushing her backwards on to the bed. 'However, there are a few questions....'

'You're serious?' she said. 'Paul's dead?' She shook her head in denial. 'He can't be dead. I came down here to find him.'

'Any special reason for that?' Dugdale asked. 'Hoping for a reconciliation, were you? Isn't that sad, Sergeant?'

Malone shifted from one foot to another. He thought his boss was being unduly harsh. 'I'd say it was sad, sir,' he said, 'there must've been some reason for them staying married all these years. Perhaps they really were getting back together.'

'You see, Vita, Sergeant Malone is a sentimentalist. I'm not, myself. I'd say your marriage never meant very much to you, and when Paul left, you never got round to making the split official. Why should you? There was nothing in it for you, was there? What interests me is why you thought there was now.'

Vita sat up straight on the edge of the bed and began to fluff up her hair. She smiled. 'What happened? How did he die?'

'He was murdered, Vita. Someone gave him a heroin overdose and made it look as though he'd killed himself.'

'Are you sure he didn't? It could've been suicide.'

'Why, do you think he killed himself because he knew you were on your way to re-establish your conjugal rights?' Dugdale said.

Malone was really shocked that his boss could say that, and then he was even more shocked when Vita laughed.

'He didn't know,' she said. 'I wanted it to be a surprise. I've been searching all over. You can check at a place called the *Hell Hole*, I think they'd remember me there.'

Malone wrote down the name, and as he did so, he recalled that one of the girls at the club had told him how careful Vita had been to establish that she was Paul's wife.

He said to Dugdale, 'That's true, sir. I spoke to someone there about Paul Meyer and she mentioned that Mrs Meyer had been in.'

In saying this, Malone knew that Dugdale would understand that he, too, had become suspicious of Vita. What she said was too planned, too pat.

Dugdale's voice took on a silky overtone that Malone recognized as a sign that he was about to come to the real point of this interview.

'You know, Vita, Sergeant Malone may believe that you rushed down to London to look for Paul because you'd been missing him all these years, but I'm not quite convinced. Didn't you think that Paul Meyer had done well for himself in London? You wanted money, didn't you?'

'How would I know he was rich? And why should I care. I've got my own business in Manchester, a club in the city centre.'

'We know your backers are about to foreclose,' Malone said quietly.

Malone's sudden contribution seemed to disconcert Vita. She said nothing.

Dugdale said, 'I think Mrs Meyer may be able to answer her own question. How would she know he was rich unless someone told her?'

Vita shrugged. She took a lipstick from the handbag lying on the bed beside her and began to colour her lips in a slightly different vivid red from the one she had been wearing.

'OK,' she said, after a long pause. 'Some drunken tart came into the club one night and started drivelling on about her love life with this rich bastard who'd been treating her bad. And then she showed me his picture and it was Paul. From the way she talked, he was rolling in it.'

'What was her name, this drunken tart?'

Vita fumbled in the handbag. 'She gave me her card. I was going to call her if I couldn't find Paul by myself. I reckoned she'd know where he was. Here it is. Sue Stockland. And here's her address. That's all I know.'

As Dugdale and Malone walked down the steps of the hotel and turned to walk back down Eversholt Street towards their car, Malone said, 'Well, that was useful.'

Dugdale, apparently lost in thought, only nodded.

Malone went on, 'At least now you've got something to talk about on your date with Miss Stockland, sir. Binge drinking in Manchester.'

Dugdale said, 'Any way you look at it, the main topic of conversation is still going to be Paul Meyer and how he suddenly turned up dead.'

19 Small Talk

Lucy found herself dialling Paul's number in what she now knew to be Sue Stockland's flat in London.

Why am I doing this? she asked herself. Do I really hope the police have got everything all wrong and Paul will answer the phone? And then she almost put the phone down when she realized that she was dialling the number simply to see what might happen. That's pathetic, she told herself, it's worse than pathetic, it's stupid. I'm ringing Paul's number because I want Sue Stockland to answer without it looking as though I actually want to talk to her.

Lucy was well aware that she was behaving like an idiot, but at the moment she was doing and thinking a lot of things which seemed to have nothing to do with what she intended.

'Is that you, Lucy?' Sue Stockland's voice asked. At least, Lucy thought, it must be Sue's voice because the telephone was in Sue's flat, although she didn't recognize this as the same woman she'd talked to a few days ago. Then, Lucy had drawn some sort of comfort from how depressed and miserable Paul's other love had sounded; now Sue sounded much more cheerful and definitely positive.

Lucy was disconcerted because when it came down to it, one of the unadmitted reasons for her to be ringing at all was to show Sue that she wasn't defeated, that she was succeeding in putting the past behind her. It was bravado. What you wanted to do was crow, Lucy told herself, so if you don't like what you hear, it serves you right.

'I almost didn't recognize your voice,' Sue was saying. 'You sound different, more grown up.'

'You sound different, too,' Lucy said. 'No, I just wanted to give you a telephone number where you can get me for a while. I've moved out of my old house and this is my temporary number. I'm staying with friends.'

'Are you going to move away?' Sue asked. 'I've thought of doing that, everything here reminds me of Paul. But it's not so easy, because I work from home and it's difficult to move a business like mine.'

'I thought you might have had his telephone taken out,' Lucy said.

'I'm going to ring BT to come to do it today. You're the last person to ring it, so that at least is the end of an era,' Sue said.

She's not the sentimental type, Lucy told herself. I wouldn't have his phone taken out.

Sue seemed to know what Lucy was thinking. 'If you think I'm trying to erase all trace of him from my life,' she said, 'you're right. Sentimental gestures are all very well, but not at the cost which BT charge for the line rental.'

Lucy wasn't sure if Sue was joking. 'It sounds as though your business is going well,' Lucy said. I can't believe this, she thought, what am I doing talking to this woman as though she and I are actually friends.

'How are you doing?' Sue asked. 'Is it getting any easier for you?'

The trouble is, Lucy thought, I really do want to talk to her. No one else understands, but she will.

Lucy found herself wondering what Sue Strickland was like. Does she look like me? she thought, Paul loved us both, so are we alike? She tried to imagine her rival, but only succeeded in picturing a slimmer, more sophisticated metropolitan version of herself.

She said to Sue, 'I still can't believe he betrayed me – us – as he did, but it doesn't seem to matter so much now. It's as though it all happened a long time ago.'

'I know enough about men to expect them to betray me,' Sue said. 'It's happened often enough before. I can't get over how I really believed it was different with Paul.'

Lucy said shyly, 'He was my first. I'd never loved anyone before him.'

'You're kidding?' Sue said. 'You can't be serious.'

''Fraid it's true. But I won't make the same mistake again,' Lucy said.

'Of course you will. You may think you'll never dare love anyone again, but you'll suddenly find you're in love and this whole business won't have taught you a thing except perhaps next time you won't sell your house to give him the money.'

'I don't know,' Lucy said, 'that's what they say about giving birth a second time, you don't get put off by the first.'

'Ughh,' Sue said, 'that's a particular form of masochism I know nothing about and care about even less.'

'You know, you could be right. About love, I mean, not giving birth,' Lucy said. She wanted Sue to ask the right question so she could tell her about Guy.

'So you've met someone else already?' Sue said. 'Really?'

Can I trust her? Lucy asked herself. She hesitated, and the moment was lost.

Sue was saying, 'Other things have obviously been happening for you. That makes it easier, when there's lots going on in your life.'

'There's certainly more going on in my life now than there ever was before,' Lucy said, and laughed.

'Me too,' Sue said. 'I concentrated on work and now other things are going on. The awful thing is, I miss Paul, but when I ask myself what I miss, there doesn't seem to have been anything there. Do you understand that, or am I going crazy?'

'Do you know, I hadn't thought it out, but that's exactly how I feel. I try to remember things to make me feel close to him, but everything just seems to melt away when I do that.'

Sue laughed, but without malice. 'Isn't that something,' she said, 'the two of us trying to remind each other why we loved him so much? What I do regret, though, is that those two monster kids of his didn't exist. It would've been some sort of revenge if they'd made him as miserable as he said they did.'

Lucy laughed with Sue, but she couldn't quite bring herself to wish there hadn't been a real Julie. She would have liked to help the poor little thing.

'Will you ring again?' Sue asked. 'I've arranged to go out on the hunt tonight, so I can't talk now, but perhaps another time...?

'Yes,' Lucy said, 'I'd like that. It's all right, isn't it? We both loved Paul and he loved us, so we must have some common ground. It helps to talk about it, it makes me feel real again. Good hunting tonight, anyway.'

'It's in the bag,' Sue said. 'You should try it, it's better than booze.'

'Oh, I know it is,' Lucy said, 'but I promise I won't do anything you wouldn't do.'

20 Just a Little Lust

Dugdale was late for his appointment with Sue Stockland, which put him on the wrong foot.

When he got to the bar where he had arranged to meet her, she wasn't there. Dugdale wasn't sure if she had been and gone, or whether she hadn't turned up herself. In either case, he needed a drink, but he ordered a mineral water.

The bar was almost deserted. Even so, he was the only man there drinking alone.

The barman took his order and asked, 'Are you Mr Dugdale?'

Dugdale nodded.

'A young lady said to give you a message if you came in. She waited for over an hour,' the barman said, looking Dugdale up and down to see what was so special about him that a stunner like Sue Stockland was prepared to wait so long for him; and then leave a message rather than storm out.

'Well,' Dugdale said, 'what was the message?'

'She said she'd wait for you at home,' the barman said. 'She said to come on over.'

That wasn't particularly good, Dugdale thought, it gave her the initiative and he had deliberately planned to meet Sue on neutral ground. He knew the way women of her sort worked on men, and he was afraid that on home ground she would have an advantage over him. She certainly had that now, when he had kept her waiting so long. He owed her an apology.

He went to her flat and she made light of his rudeness.

'I understand about work,' she said, taking his arm and leading him into the sitting-room. 'I know how things can get out of control. Don't worry, I've got a Thai take-away keeping hot in the oven.'

Dugdale was hungry, but he demurred. She laughed at him.

'Don't worry,' she said, 'I'm not trying to compromise you. I've got to eat and I thought that if we're going to talk about Paul, we might eat as well as talk.'

They ate at the kitchen table. She opened a bottle of white wine and then sat back in her chair.

'Not for me, thanks,' Dugdale said. He thought she might press him, but she didn't.

'Are we avoiding the subject of Paul?' she asked.

'No,' Dugdale said. 'But first there's something I've got to ask you.'

'Fire away,' she said.

Dugdale reached into the inner pocket of his jacket and brought out a photograph.

'Do you recognize this woman?' he asked.

Sue took the photo from him and looked at it closely.

'Yes,' she said, 'sort of. I mean, I don't know her personally. She looks like the woman I talked to last week in Manchester. She ran a bar there. But then I suppose she looks like a lot of women behind bars in clubs in Manchester. It was called something to do with hats. The *Sombrero*, something like that.'

'The *Fedora*,' Dugdale said.

'That sounds right. I don't remember now. What about her? Who is she?'

'Did you talk to her about Paul?'

'I guess I did. He was on my mind.'

'Did you mention his name?'

'No, I don't think so. I may have said Paul in passing, but not his surname. I didn't identify him, if that's what you mean. Actually, I was a bit the worse for wear, so I'm not sure, but I don't think so. Oh, I think I may've shown her a photo. Why do you want to know?'

'Oh, it was something that came up, that's all. This woman didn't happen to reciprocate with reminiscences about bastards I have loved, did she?'

'No, she didn't. She didn't say much at all, she listened. I needed someone to sound off to, and she filled the bill. That's her job. She works behind a bar, for God's sake, that's what happens. People don't go into clubs like that to listen to details of the barmaid's love life.' Then Sue smiled at him and added, 'Sorry, perhaps men do. And then they show them the photos of their kids they keep in their wallets, except the barmaid's looking at his wad, not the baby picture. Is that what gets you going?'

'I should go,' Dugdale said.

'Don't be silly. I haven't even started to tell you why I'm sure Lucy Drake killed Paul. We'll have coffee in the sitting-room, these kitchen chairs are uncomfortable.'

In the sitting-room she gestured Dugdale to sit on the sofa. When he had, she sat close beside him.

Damn, he thought, I fell into that one.

'Exactly which night are we talking about?' he asked.

'God, you don't let things ride, do you? Let's see. I had to go to Manchester the day Paul asked me to get the money he needed. I thought he was pissed off because, being in Manchester, I couldn't get it until the next day. I'd said I'd meet him, but I couldn't, of course. I left him messages. The next day I got the money. But I never gave it to him, did I? He didn't come home that night and in the morning I reported him missing.'

All of a sudden she began to weep. Dugdale waited, but she wept on. Embarrassed, he offered her his handkerchief, but she slumped towards him and buried her face against his chest. He could feel a patch of hot wetness spreading on his shirt.

Awkwardly, he patted her on the shoulder, but the volume of

her weeping grew. Then he felt her arms creeping round his neck and her hot, damp, mouth against his ear.

'Hold me,' she whispered, her lips moving on his neck. 'Please, just for a moment, don't let go of me.'

He patted her again and then tried to pull away as her mouth covered his and he felt her hand slide inside his fly.

'No,' he tried to say against her thrusting tongue, 'I can't, I'm a married man.'

'It's just a little lust,' Sue said, 'I shan't tell if you don't.' She pulled her top over her head and thrust her naked breasts into his face.

Dugdale had no chance to put up more than token resistance in the face of her lasciviousness, no matter how much Sergeant Malone would disapprove.

21 The Tattooed Man

Malone came into Dugdale's office the next morning. His boss was leaning back in his chair with his eyes shut and his feet on his desk.

Malone asked, 'What did Miss Stockland think happened in the Paul Meyer case?'

'We can be pretty sure,' Dugdale said, 'that Vita heard from Sue Stockland, that Paul was alive, rich and possibly contemplating marriage.'

'Do they know each other? Vita and the Stockland woman? That's a turn-up for the books.'

'No, it was happenstance. Sue showed Vita a photo of her lover and Vita recognized Paul. But Vita doesn't know Sue, except as a drunken and complaining girlfriend, and Sue has no idea who Vita is.'

'You didn't tell her?'

'I didn't get much chance even to ask her questions,' Dugdale said. 'She's a very emotional woman, and she's the type who gets pretty clingy if you open up raw wounds.'

Malone was about to say that he hadn't thought Sue Stockland was the clingy emotional type, but he saw how Dugdale's neck reddened above his tight shirt collar and stopped himself.

'God, I hate it when women are involved in a case like this,' Dugdale said. 'At least you can ask a man a question and he lies or tells the truth and you get a good idea which. But women lie because they're just congenital liars, and they don't even know they're doing it. They're convinced that the truth is whatever they think it is. How in hell are we supposed to deal with them?'

'Don't talk to them,' Malone said, 'watch what they do without them knowing. They give themselves away. I've learnt that from being married. I don't know if it's the same when you're not married and they think they might be in with a chance.'

'But I tell them I'm married,' Dugdale said. 'It doesn't seem to make any difference to them. I think it's me, I don't seem to know how to say no.'

Malone laughed. 'That's good,' he said, 'the counselling service might be able to fit you into a course of assertiveness training,' Malone said, and added, 'Sir.'

'Well, what is it, Malone?' Dugdale said. 'You must've had a better reason for coming in here than trying to find out if I spent the night with Sue Stockland.'

'I don't want to know any such thing,' Malone said, apparently shocked. 'I came to bring you up to speed with the investigation into Paul Meyer's death. We've another possible suspect.'

'Please tell me it's a man. I've known all along there should be a male suspect.'

'Well,' Malone said, 'this could be the one. A newspaper-seller with a pitch near Tottenham Court Road tube station was on his way to work on the morning we found Meyer's body. The station wasn't open, and he ducked into an alleyway for a slash. Then he saw a man come out of a side door behind a sandwich bar.'

'And? Was it the alley where we found the corpse?'

'No, but not far from it. The newspaper-vendor saw in the papers that a body had been found, and later that day he told a constable on the beat because he thought there might be something in it.'

'A reward, you mean?'

'The constable didn't say. He only mentioned it to CID because he was the one who'd found the body earlier, but only after he found out who had an office behind that side door: the office was Paul Meyer's.'

Dugdale dropped his feet to the floor with a crash. 'Was it indeed? Recommend that constable for transfer to CID, he's brighter than we are. Have we searched the office?'

'Nothing there except a table, a chair, a pile of telephone directories and a few box files. I've got someone looking through these for anything helpful. Oh, and a mobile phone with no messages; the last call on it was to a pizza take-away, made twenty-four hours before the estimated time of death.'

'No safe?'

'No. One thing, though, the newspaper-seller recognized the man in the alley.'

'The hell he did?'

'He'd seen him earlier the day before. He'd come up to his pitch and asked if he knew a sandwich bar up one of the streets nearby. The vendor noticed him because he thought from the way he talked that he was a Geordie, but the man didn't seem to know what he was talking about. He'd got a dragon tattooed on the back of his neck.'

'A dragon? Now we're getting somewhere,' Dugdale said. 'I know a man with a tattoo like that.'

'A dragon on the back of the neck?' Malone said. 'There must be hundreds, it's hardly conclusive evidence.'

'We've got to start from somewhere,' Dugdale said. 'The man I'm thinking about is a pro. He's a right bastard called Jed Mallet; used to be a boxer and a few years ago he was working as an all-purpose enforcer for Saul Kramer.'

'Big Saul? Could he be behind this?'

'Why not?'

Dugdale was angry with himself. He'd known that Paul Meyer had worked for Big Saul in Manchester, but he'd failed to make the connection between Meyer and the Saul Kramer who was now behind a fair amount of organized crime in London's West End.

'You could be right,' he told Malone, 'there's not much on the shady side in Soho that he isn't behind. Get a move on, Malone, and find out where he's operating from these days. We'll pay Big Saul a visit.'

22 The Pressure Mounts

Lucy drove slowly up the drive towards her former home. Both Tara and Quentin Burns had left for work earlier, leaving her alone in their house. But being alone in other people's homes wasn't like being alone at all and Lucy wanted to be on her own for a while. People were too bloody kind, they were trying to take her mind off her shattered life, but Lucy knew that the only way she was going to get back on track was to put Paul's death and the loss of her home behind her, and take control of her future. She hadn't had a moment to think about what was happening to her while she'd been staying at the Burnses'.

She was embarrassed now by the way she'd reacted when Maxine and the Burnses had attacked her about Guy Dugdale. She realized that she'd gone a bit over the top giving the impression that her handsome policeman could be the love of her life. The way her friends had been so suspicious and negative about him had made her defensive. She'd simply wanted to shut them up and stop making her even more confused than she already was. And perhaps she did feel a little guilty that she might be using Guy as a way of sorting herself out. He was good-looking and straightforward and they had a great time together and that was what she wanted now. But perhaps she was trifling with his affections, as her father used to say about certain of his parishioners who were involved with insincere men. As far as Lucy was concerned, the future was something else and she had too much going on in her life at the moment to think about Guy as a part of that.

I simply don't know, she said to herself, I don't know what I feel. I'm out of my depth when it comes to love, I don't know what to do, all I've ever learned about love came out of books until I met Paul and I made a complete fool of myself with him.

Lucy wanted to talk all this through with someone who would understand. Her friends were hopeless; Max would disapprove of everything and Tara saw everything in terms of what was going on between her and Quentin. No, there was only one person Lucy really wanted to confide in, and that was Sue Stockland. Sue didn't know her, Sue must be at least dispassionate if not openly hostile and she didn't seem to be the sentimental type. Lucy was sure that Sue Stockland knew what she was talking about when it came down to love and that stuff. There was no point in discussing her feelings with Guy because he was involved.

She tried to imagine Guy here with her, dressed in old cords and a waxed jacket with a tweed cap and muddy gumboots. The picture was so incongruous that she laughed. Guy would never make an authentic countryman. And I'd never fit up in London, not permanently, Lucy told herself, but there's no need to think about that now. At the moment being together is what counts, wherever we are.

But as she drove up the dappled lane, hearing the sound of birds singing in the hedges through the open car window, with a view of wooded hills stretching to the sky, it seemed to her that this was a wonderful place to be and that surely even Guy would see that.

It was the sort of morning that suited the Devon countryside. The higgledy-piggledy fields were marked out by dry stone walls like the random joins of a jigsaw puzzle, very clear after rain earlier. There was a brisk breeze and as Lucy drove she could see the tracks of the sun across the distant valley as the racing clouds seemed to play football with it.

Lucy knew that her old home had been partly demolished. Her furniture had been taken into storage. All signs of her occupation and her father's, almost all of her life, had been obliterated. But Quentin had mentioned that the work was now stalled for a few days because the builders had found asbestos somewhere on the site and were waiting for a specialist to remove it. The site was deserted, there would be no workmen to bother her.

If I don't go and see what they've done, I don't think I'm going to believe it's not still there to pick up where I left off, she told herself, and then thought, What made me do it, how could I throw everything away like that?

She found it curious that the death of Paul, who had filled her life – or at least her weekends – for so long, had paled to insignificance in comparison with the sale of her home and with it her place in village life. Paul no longer seemed as though he had ever been real. And, of course, he wasn't real – not the Paul she'd thought he was. He was like a character in a book she'd been really involved with until she finished reading it.

I loved him, she said to herself, but then it was as though he evaporated, and loving him wasn't any more real than he was. It isn't him fooling me that's so hard to take, but how could I have fooled myself like that?

What she found most difficult to deal with, though, was the loss of her central role in the village. She felt that buying the cottage by the church and staying on among her friends would restore the continuity of decades of belonging. She would still belong in the parish, still be the old vicar's daughter, on the electoral register and paying council tax. But without the background of the old family home, the part she would play would be passive; as a participant, true, but no longer a defining force in the life of the community.

I'll settle down here again, she thought, but things will be different. That's good, it's how it should be. I've spent too long just carrying on as a leftover of other people's lives: now I'll build one from scratch for myself. The cottage by the church will be my first real home of my own and as there's enough money left over, I can go into partnership with Quentin. We can build up the business together and I'll invest the rest in fixed interest bonds to bring in a bit extra.

Lucy turned off the main road into the drive prepared to see the old house reduced to rubble. She hadn't expected the façade to be unaltered. Her old home looked exactly the same from the drive as if she'd been able to turn the clock back and was coming home a fortnight ago, or a month, or twenty years.

But there was now a rusty old caravan parked on the lawn, a lawn which had been her father's pride and joy; and the herbaceous border was a fire site, but otherwise, from the drive, nothing seemed to have changed.

Lucy walked through the front door. At once what lay behind that stately façade was proof that her past lay in ruins. She felt that she had stepped through a film set.

The internal walls were gone, or remained as stunted heaps of rubble. The once majestic staircase hung by a thread from part of a skeletal floor on the vanished landing. Strips of stained paper and fragments of white plaster were all that remained to show the house had ever boasted wallpaper, cornices or decorative panelling. And everywhere was a sour stench of damp and dust.

Lucy made her way across the muddy hallway, where the original Victorian tiled floor had been ripped up and tipped out of the back of the house on to a heap in the corner of the cobbled courtyard. She tried in her mind's eye to conjure up the rooms she had lived in. A gaping hole in the remains of an outside wall had been the drawing-room fireplace; the earth-covered Aga standing defiant in a heap of broken lathes and crumbled plaster was all that was left of the kitchen. Lucy wondered what had happened to those owls in the spare room whose old-man snores had kept her awake at night.

Everything about her life here now seemed to have happened a long time ago. But it was only a matter of days.

It's over, Lucy told herself, it's over and I can't go back.

She went over to where the back door had been, opening out on to a courtyard surrounded by outbuildings. This must be where they found the asbestos, she thought; the demolition had scarcely started. She looked over the half door of a stable block where her great-grandfather had kept his carriage horses, then went in. As a child she'd kept a pony in one of these stalls. There was a loft above which she remembered as being full of sweet-smelling loose hay; that was when they'd made their own hay in the paddock at the back of the house.

She'd left the stable door open and a shaft of sunlight fell across the flag floor that had always been kept scrubbed clean years before. Leaning against the wall of one of the stalls, she watched the dust dancing in the sun's rays and thought of those long-ago days in the field turning the hay with old-fashioned two-pronged pitchforks, the mauve, yellow and white wild flowers drying in the wind, and the colours of the various grasses when the hay was ready to put into cocks before being heaved on to the flat-bed wagons with hurdles lashed back and front to stop the hay spilling. So many different shades of green!

The ray of sunlight disappeared. It was as though someone had switched off a light. Lucy looked to see what was blocking the sunshine, and she saw the outline of a man.

He seemed enormous, black against the sky behind him.

Lucy thought he must be one of the builders.

'I'm sorry,' she said, 'I suppose I'm trespassing. I used to live here.'

She found the way he stood motionless in the doorway somehow threatening.

'I'm going,' she said, and began to walk towards him. She hoped that he would move aside, or at least say something.

'Big Saul wants what's 'is,' the man said. He turned his head and she saw the tattooed head of a dragon on the back of his neck. He had other tattoos as well, even on the backs of his hands.

'I'm sorry,' she said, trying to keep her voice steady, 'I don't know who Big Saul is.'

Far from retreating, the tattooed man came through the half-door and bolted it behind him. 'You knew Paul Meyer, didn't you?'

Lucy's mouth was dry. She tried to speak, but could only nod her head.

'Then you must know Big Saul,' the tattooed man said. He exuded such menace that Lucy saw no reason to question his dubious logic.

'Big Saul wants 'is money,' the tattooed man said, ''e sent me 'ere to get it.'

Lucy cringed away from him.

'You going to give it to me nice and easy?' he said. 'Or the 'ard way?' He smiled at her when he said this and Lucy recoiled at what looked to her like a toothless snarl. This freakish threat daunted Lucy, who had often faced the jaws of ferocious dogs in the course of her life without a qualm .

'I haven't got Big Saul's money,' she said. She tried not to show panic, but she knew she sounded scared.

'So it's the 'ard way, is it? I 'ope you don't live to regret that,' the man said, and from the way he said it she knew he was glad she was going to try to make things difficult.

'No,' Lucy said and she heard the horrible fear in her own voice, 'honestly, I haven't got the money – any money.' She had a brainwave. 'I gave it to Paul,' she said. 'He took it to London with him.'

Backing away from him, she tripped and fell against the wall. The big man moved forward and grabbed her by the neck, holding her upright with his fingers hooked under her chin, blocking her throat. He pressed more tightly as she clawed help-lessly at his face, trying to make him loosen his grip.

She made strangled noises and he loosened his grip slightly. 'You ready to talk now?' he said.

Her eyes felt as though they were going to burst out of their sockets. His fingers clamped on her throat seemed to tighten like a vice.

'I gave Paul the money,' she tried to say, 'he had it with him when he went to London.'

She could smell his breath as he thrust his face into hers. He'd been eating garlic and her head began to swim. She couldn't focus her eyes properly and, as her knees started to sag, the patterns on the tattoos which covered even his fingers began to merge and dance in front of her.

He pulled her towards him and shook her. 'Where?' he hissed in her face. 'Where is it?'

She tried to loosen his grip with both her hands. 'Can't breathe,' she managed to whisper.

He dropped her so that she staggered against the side of the stall.

'Don't waste my bleeding time,' he said, 'if you tell me, maybe I won't kill you.'

'You can't kill me here,' she said, cowering away from him. 'The builders will come soon.'

'No, they won't,' he said, as though he were talking to a naughty child. 'They won't be 'ere for days and they won't find where I'll 'ide you that soon, neither. Where did Meyer take the money?'

'I don't know,' Lucy said. 'Honestly, I don't know.'

She watched him flex his huge fingers and reach for her again.

'No,' she said, whimpering, 'no, please. I'll tell you everything I know. He lived with a woman called Sue Stockland in London. She must be in the telephone book. Perhaps he took the money there.'

Somewhere in the distance a dog started to bark. The sound seemed to break the tattooed man's concentration. He pushed Lucy aside.

'If you're wrong,' he said, 'you're dead.'

He turned and went out. The ray of sunlight streamed back across the stable floor. Lucy listened as the sound of the tattooed man's footsteps on the cobbles faded and died.

She gradually got back to her feet. Her throat was painful, and she was shaking with fear. Slowly, she staggered out of the stable and made her way back through the house.

She was suddenly struck by what she had done.

My God, she thought, I've got to warn that woman. She may have had a hand in killing Paul, but if that thug gets to her, I'll have killed her.

She ran to her car to find her mobile phone. She couldn't remember Sue's number. She knew exactly where she had written it on an old envelope and she'd put it down somewhere, but where? And the number of Paul's phone was discontinued. Perhaps Directory Inquiries could find Sue's number, even though she didn't know the address. But when she tried to ring them, the mobile battery had run out.

Lucy drove as fast as she could to the Burnses' house. Tara and Quentin were still at work. She started to look in the London telephone directory, but there were too many Stocklands, and she wasn't familiar enough with London to know which might be Sue's.

She started dialling one of the Stocklands, then stopped and put the phone down. This was a waste of time. And then she had a vision of herself on Friday nights, ringing Paul in London to try to find out if he was on his way. She remembered how she had hated to hear his voice on the answering machine, telling her he wasn't there, to leave a message.

I bet she didn't have it disconnected, Lucy thought. She knew what I was thinking about keeping it as a memento, she felt sentimental about it too.

Paul's phone rang on and on. Perhaps she did have it cut off, Lucy thought, and because she was a little disappointed because she had misjudged Sue, she persisted and let it ring on.

Then at last a man answered, and in a light, silvery voice said, 'Who is this?'

'My name is Lucy Drake,' she said, and heard her voice quivering with panic. She tried to calm down so that he could understand her. 'I need to speak to Sue Stockland,' she said.

The man on the line sounded breathless and shocked himself. 'She isn't here,' he said, 'this isn't her telephone. You're ringing a dead man's number.'

'Please,' Lucy said, 'I don't know who you are, but please give her a message. It's really important.'

'Well, give it to me, then, and I'll tell her,' the man with the silvery voice said.

It crossed Lucy's mind that Sue, too, had a new man in her life.

'Please, tell her there's a man looking for her and if he finds her, he'll hurt her. He's got a dragon tattooed on his neck, and tattoos on his hands, and someone called Big Saul sent him to get Paul's money.'

Lucy heard a stifled gulp on the line. Then the phone went dead.

23 Big Saul in Soho

In the car taking Dugdale and Malone to visit Big Saul Kramer, the Detective Chief Inspector sat hunched beside the detective constable who was driving them and stared sightlessly at the crowds in the streets. He looked ridiculous in the passenger seat, Malone thought, far too big and broad; he needed the steering wheel to give the impression that he had a function in a car.

Their driver knew the back alleys, and in spite of heavy traffic the journey from Victoria to Soho only took a few minutes. When they stopped across the entrance to an alley off Frith Street, Dugdale grunted as he got out of the car.

'You could moonlight as a licensed taxi driver,' he said to the constable. 'You'd probably make more in one shift than you do in a week with us.' He turned and walked up the alley.

'That was a compliment,' Malone said to the constable, who looked as though he thought Dugdale was giving him the sack. 'Pick us up in half an hour.'

Malone hurried after Dugdale, who suddenly stopped and turned to look back the way he'd come.

'We've been here before,' he said.

'Yes, sir,' Malone said. 'You had your first sexual encounter with a tart against the wall here. Or somewhere very like it.'

Dugdale gave him a hard look. 'More to the point, we found that bloody body here, didn't we?'

'Paul Meyer's body? Yes, sir, I think it was here. Here, or somewhere close by and almost identical.'

'Stop pussyfooting about, it was here,' Dugdale said. 'What do you make of that?'

'Nothing. Most alleys in this part of London must've had bodies found in them over the years,' Malone said. 'It just happens to be where Saul Kramer has an office.'

'Why would he dump a body he'd had killed on his own doorstep?'

Malone thought for a moment. 'Well, perhaps it was a deliberate ploy to put us off the scent because we'd know he wouldn't do such a stupid thing? They took a lot of trouble to make it look like suicide.'

Dugdale said nothing, but he turned and walked on up the alley to the doorway which led to Big Saul's office.

'Careful where you tread,' he said, 'the sort of germs that breed in these alleys can probably penetrate police issue boots.'

'But not some coppers' skins,' muttered Malone under his breath.

Dugdale gave him another hard look. 'This isn't a job for sensitive flowers, Sergeant,' he said. 'Put it down to the company we keep. Like the bugger we're about to see. Is this your first time?'

'With Big Saul? I've never met him. I know him by reputation, of course. But he's never done time. He may be a model citizen....'

'... Except for the company he keeps? Sure, and pigs might be spreading bird flu. We just haven't been able to get any evidence to stand up in court. In cases against Big Saul, when we've had witnesses their life expectancy goes down to zero. There's not been a survivor yet.'

A moth-eaten cat with blazing green eyes suddenly leaped out of a pile of bursting bin bags with an outraged snarl and fled up the alley. Malone jumped.

'Oh dear,' Dugdale said, 'the Kramer family pet has left home. And look, someone's left the door open.'

The lock gave so easily when he put his shoulder to the door that this was almost true.

'You know this isn't legal, don't you?' Malone said. 'We've no right to break down doors!' But he clattered after Dugdale up the narrow, uncarpeted staircase to the fourth-floor.

'It must be difficult to take Mr Kramer by surprise,' Dugdale said, musing aloud. 'Imagine being on nights trying to sleep in one of these bedsits with Kramer's visitors coming and going all day on those bare stairs.'

A door on the landing opened and a man nearly as tall as Dugdale himself came out to meet them. His broken nose and beetling eyebrows looked out of place with his neat pin-stripe suit and discreet silk tie. He said, 'How can I help you?'

'We're police officers,' Malone said, preparing to show his ID card.

'Of course you are. I'm Saul Kramer. What can I do for you?'

'We want to ask you some questions about Paul Meyer,' Dugdale said.

Big Saul turned and they followed him back into his office. There was thick carpet on the floor but the room was dimly lit and the only window was so thick with the grime of years that the watery sunlight outside could not penetrate the glass. The place was unbearably hot and Malone began to feel he might fall down if he couldn't sit.

Big Saul seemed to consider. 'Paul Meyer? Wasn't that the young man who committed suicide in the street outside here? I know the police are doing their best, but these drug addicts are getting out of hand.'

'He worked for you at one time. In Manchester,' Dugdale said.

Big Saul's expression did not change. He seemed to be trying to remember.

'No, it doesn't come to mind. It's many years since I spent much time in Manchester, though I still have an affection for the dirty old city. As I expect you do yourself, Inspector?'

'Did you know him?' Dugdale asked. It was clear from his tone that he didn't intend to chat about old times.

'He owed me money. A lot of money. I wondered at the time if perhaps worrying about that might have caused him to take his own life.'

'Why should you think that, Mr Kramer? Were you putting pressure on him?'

Big Saul laughed. 'There's nothing threatening about asking a debtor to repay his debts.'

'Did you see him that night? Did he come here?'

'Not that I know of. I didn't see him. And why should he? He'd told my agent that he could get the money the next day. He was adamant that he could. There was no pressure on him.'

'Do you know his wife? Has she been here?'

Did Big Saul's eyes flicker with interest? At least Dugdale thought so, Malone wasn't sure.

'I didn't know he was married,' Big Saul said. 'Did the poor young man have children? So often when young men get into debt it's because they have children.'

'When you say Paul Meyer owed you a lot of money, what sort of sums are we talking about?'

Big Saul cupped his hand over his mouth and apparently started to pick his teeth. The hand seemed to have a life of its own at the end of the pin-striped sleeve. It was like some animal, covered in coarse black hair. Or perhaps a tarantula, Malone thought, a tarantula with thick bristly legs and a glaring eye which was the stone in the man's signet ring.

'I think I'll keep my client's confidence on that,' Big Saul said. 'But why are you asking me these questions? Surely when a man dies of a huge heroin overdose, it's either suicide or an accident?'

'How did you know he died of a heroin overdose?' Malone asked. He hoped they could finish this soon. The heat was stifling. It was making it difficult for him to concentrate.

Big Saul laughed. 'When someone dies on one's doorstep, of

course one is curious, even in a place like this,' he said. 'I asked the constable on duty. He said he'd found the body with a syringe clamped in his dead hand.'

There was a short silence. Then Big Saul said, 'I hope you won't think me rude, but I've an appointment I must keep.... I take it that you think Meyer was murdered – otherwise why would you be investigating his death? As you're here, I presume you suspect me. I'm quite insulted, actually; what kind of murderer dumps the body of his victim on his own doorstep?'

Dugdale opened the door and a wave of beautiful cold air flowed into the room. Speaking over his shoulder as he went out, as though he were making casual conversation, Dugdale said, 'Incidentally, we know of two women who raised the money Meyer needed to pay you. I wonder what he did with it, if he didn't give it to you?'

Outside in the alley at last, Malone shut the street door and leaned back against it, breathing in the damp air.

'We've no evidence against him at all,' he said, hoping that Dugdale wouldn't notice how the hot room had affected him.

'True,' Dugdale said. 'That bastard must take homeopathic doses of rat poison to thin his blood, working in a room that hot.'

'What's our next step?'

'That's up to Mr Big Saul Kramer. I baited the hook by letting slip that the money exists; lets see if he goes after it. We wait and we watch.'

Malone looked at him in amazement. 'But doesn't that put those two women – Lucy Drake and Sue Stockland – into the line of fire? They never got to give Meyer the money. Big Saul will go after them.'

'Kramer wants the money, harming them wouldn't get him anywhere.' Dugdale showed no sign of concern.

'My God, sir, you can't do this. The man may be a killer.' Malone would have liked to say straight out, if he dared, that lawyers mightn't worry too much about using witnesses as bait, but it wasn't what policemen did.

'So we'll put a watch on them,' Dugdale said. 'Come on, Malone, we're trying to catch a killer, and you can't make an omelette without breaking eggs.'

In spite of his bullish tone, Dugdale looked sheepish. He knew exactly what Malone was thinking. But, he told himself, if he couldn't provoke Big Saul to criminal action which would give them evidence to put that slimy bastard behind bars, there was no chance at all of making him pay for anything he had done so far. Which probably included getting Paul Meyer killed. Manchester was a long time ago, but old scores died hard and Dugdale still had a few to settle with Big Saul Kramer.

'Anyway,' he said to Malone, 'if those women scare Big Saul as much as they terrify me, you've nothing to worry about.'

'But suppose they don't,' Malone said. 'That's what I worry about.'

24 A Killer Comes Calling

Sue Stockland came into her flat and put several bags of shopping down inside the door. Then she kicked off her shoes and went to the sitting-room to pour herself a drink.

She opened a bottle of wine and the pop of the cork brought a muffled shriek from behind the sofa.

Sue took the bottle by the neck, ready to dash it against the mantelpiece to make a weapon.

'Who's there?' she said. 'Come out.'

She waited. Then Neville's scared white face appeared from behind the sofa.

'Darling, don't shoot. It's me, Neville, your friend.'

Sue wanted to laugh, but something about his expression stopped her. He looked as though he had been really frightened.

'Neville, what's happened? Why are you hiding behind the sofa?'

'Oh, my God, I thought you were a homicidal maniac coming to kill me. Give me a drink, quick, before I faint dead away.'

Sue had had a hard day at work and the shock of finding Neville cowering in her sitting-room like a thief gave way to indignation.

'What are you playing at, you idiot? You frightened me half to death? There aren't any homicidal maniacs here.'

'Darling, don't panic, but someone rang Paul's private phone and said there's a man coming to kill you.'

Sue took a glass of wine, then sat on the sofa looking down over the back at her trembling friend.

'Oh, Neville, what's got into you? Who would ring Paul's number now? It must've been a wrong number.'

Neville grabbed the top of the sofa and pulled himself upright. He looked really pale. Sue could see he had been genuinely terrified.

'Sue, please believe me. We've got to escape. This woman rang and wanted to speak to you and she said there's a vicious thug coming who's going to kill you and he's covered in dragons and he wants Paul's money.'

'Covered with dragons? What's that mean? Neville, are you on something?'

'He's covered in tattoos. One of them's a dragon. On his neck.'

He sat beside her on the sofa. He was almost in tears. She could see that he was trembling.

She gave him her drink and got up to pour herself a new glass, then brought the bottle with her to refill Neville's. She put her hand on his arm.

'It's all right, there's no one coming to kill me, darling,' Sue said. Oh God, she thought, if he's back on drugs, what am I supposed to do? She gripped his arm and shook it. 'Pull yourself together and tell me what happened,' she said. 'Who was this woman? There must be some misunderstanding. What money? Paul didn't have any money, he was trying to borrow some from me when he died. If he was in debt and some criminal was putting the screws on him, they'd be looking for places he might have stashed money, not for daft women who were prepared to lend it to him.'

'They might think you know what he did with it.'

Thank God, Sue told herself, he's not on drugs, he's just scared out of his mind, poor little wimp.

'He never got it,' Sue said, trying to reassure him. 'I was going to give it to him the day he died.'

Sue smiled at him, and leaned over to ruffle his Hint of a Tint chestnut hair.

'Maybe I'm beginning to have an idea why he wanted it,

though,' she said. 'Paul's long-lost wife has turned up and maybe she knows something we don't.'

'But even a long-lost wife couldn't know his number here, could she? This woman was trying to warn you. Why should Paul's ex-wife do that? What's her name, anyway?'

'Vita. And apparently she's not ex-. She's still Mrs Meyer. Perhaps she's trying to frighten me into telling her if I gave the money to him and what he did with it, so she pretends I'm in danger and that she's my friend.'

'Well that wasn't the name the woman on the phone said.'

'She gave her name? What was it?'

Neville made a helpless wringing gesture with his hands. 'That's the trouble, I've forgotten. I was so scared, and it was one of those names you don't remember. You know, all hissing sounds, like Suzie or Sally or Izzy....'

Sue gave him a sharp look. 'Could she've said Lucy?'

Neville jumped up in excitement. 'That's it, Lucy.' He sat down again, looking deflated but much less scared. 'Do you actually *know* anyone called Lucy?'

'Paul did,' Sue said, and something almost menacing in her tone made Neville give her a sharp look.

Sue smiled. 'I spoke to her on the phone once,' she said. 'Lucy Drake. She's a hysteric. She told my policeman that she thought I killed Paul.'

For some reason she couldn't quite fathom, Sue didn't want Neville to know that she and Lucy had talked several times on the phone. He'd be jealous, she told herself.

Neville had lost his pale look of terror. 'Ooh, did she really say that? What a bitch!'

Sue shrugged, dismissing Lucy with the gesture.

'She's just some sort of hick who got tangled up with a scheme of Paul's. She's not worth bothering about.'

'You mean there isn't a homicidal maniac about to burst in and strangle you?'

'Oh, Neville, drop it. Lucy's nothing, nobody, just some sort of drama queen. No one even took her seriously when she accused me of murdering Paul. Reading between the lines, I'd say Guy thinks she's a bit unhinged. Actually, I think she's raving mad and she could easily have killed Paul herself because she found out about me and him. She's obviously insanely jealous.'

'Oh, it's Guy now, is it? Do you have to call him Detective Chief Inspector when he's asking you intimate questions?'

'Don't be silly, Neville. He questioned Lucy Drake as part of the investigation into Paul's death, that's all. Paul had conned her into giving him money, I think. What's between Guy and me hasn't got anything to do with that.'

'So there is something between the two of you?'

Sue's face lighted up. 'Oh, Neville, he's unbelievable. He's such a gent. When he looks at me with those deep dark brown eyes of his, it makes me feel I'd do anything for him. You know, he's the first man I've ever known who looks like a film star and is actually shy.'

'Most men I know would be shy, the way you come on to them when in the grip of lust,' Neville said.

'You're just jealous,' she said.

'Well, he's talked to you about this Lucy, but I wonder what this Guy of yours said to Lucy Drake about you, have you thought of that?'

Sue wanted to drop the subject of Lucy Drake. It irritated her that a bumpkin like Lucy had been convincing enough, in accusing her of Paul's murder, to make Guy feel he was justified in asking her questions about her relationship with Paul. She'd laid that to rest, but it was downright annoying for Neville to suggest that Guy could think of her and Lucy Drake in anything like the same terms.

'Strictly between ourselves, darling, what have you done with the cash you raised to fund Paul's virtual sons' horrible human rehab programme?'

Sue smiled at him. 'Why would I tell you that? If you want a loan, ask the bank.'

Neville had often thought she was profligate, but so far, he'd taken it for granted that the money she spent so freely was always someone else's. He had known Sue a long time and he had always accepted that she had a penchant for rich men. But when it came down to her own money, before this business with Paul, he had thought she would be quite miserly.

'You're such a cynic,' Neville said. He sounded sad. 'If you really want to know,' he added, 'I asked because if I knew where you had put it, when our unwelcome guest arrives I could tell him where to find it and he won't hurt us.'

'Oh, shut up, Neville, the only homicidal maniac in this situation is Lucy Drake herself.'

At that moment, there was a loud knocking at the front door.

'Oh, my God!' Neville whispered, 'he's here.'

Sue stood up. She was startled, but she put on a show of bravado.

'Don't be ridiculous, Neville. How would he get up here without Ted seeing him and ringing up? Even Ted would be suspicious of a man with dragon tattoos everywhere.'

She strode to open the door.

'Don't,' Neville whispered, 'don't open it.'

'Who is it?' Sue called.

'It's Ted, Miss.'

It was Ted. She recognized his voice.

'Stay where you are, it's only Ted,' Sue told Neville. She'd rather Ted didn't know that Neville was there. It wasn't that there was anything to hide; Sue simply had the habit of secrecy even when it wasn't necessary. In business, she had a reputation for obsessional discretion, which was useful.

She went into the hall and opened the door. Ted stood there, strangely stiff and immobile. Behind him was another man, a man almost as broad as he was tall. For a second, Sue thought he was wearing some sort of multi-coloured body stocking under his t-shirt and jeans, then she saw that his body was covered in tattoos. He stood at attention behind Ted, looking like an art nouveau frame for a portrait of the little porter.

'What is it, Ted?' Sue asked. 'Who is this man?'

The tattooed man thrust Ted forward through the door and followed him quickly into the flat. He slammed the door behind him. Ted, kneeling where he had fallen, whimpered.

The tattooed man held a small but horribly authentic-looking revolver to the back of Ted's head.

'I'm sorry, Miss,' the porter whispered. 'He made me do it.'

Sue was surprised at how calm she felt. And then she realized that she was angry. All the maternal instincts she'd never thought she had were boiling up with anger at this tattooed ape. Ted didn't deserve this treatment. All he could do was cower at his assailant's feet, and Sue felt humiliated for him. He couldn't defend himself. He was a poor, ordinary, put-upon little man who was easy prey for this thug to bully.

For the first time Sue knew without thinking about it that she had bullied him herself and shame fuelled her anger. She knew Ted; she knew how many hours he put in each day at his desk in the hall downstairs; she knew he had trouble with his knees and that his back was bad and he got bad colds every winter and hardly ever took time off sick because the people who lived in 'his' flats needed him to keep their lives running smoothly.

'Don't worry, Ted,' Sue said, fixing the tattooed man with an icy stare, 'I know there was nothing you could do. You hadn't any choice. He's a bloody bully.'

She saw, on the tattooed man's bull neck, a dragon in the act of spitting fire.

She gave him a supercilious smile at the absurdity of it, but then the tattooed man hit Ted with the butt of the pistol and Ted went down with a small, sad sigh and lay still.

'You bastard,' Sue screamed, 'why did you have to do that?'

'Shut up,' the man said.

He smiled at her, and it seemed to her he was licking his lips in anticipation. She saw his toothless gums and she thought she was going to be sick.

He lunged towards her, trying to grab her, but she was too quick for him and jumped out of his way.

He stood back, raising his arms in mock surrender.

'I've come for Big Saul's money,' he said. 'Give me the money and I'll go easy.'

'Get out,' she said, snarling at him.

She kicked out at his crotch, but he caught her foot and tipped her backwards on to the floor. My bloody big feet, she thought.

Then he came for her. She screamed.

She saw Neville's terror-stricken face appear behind her attacker's shoulder. His right arm was raised, holding aloft a brass reading lamp from the sitting-room. He brought it down on the dragon tattoo on the back of the man's neck.

Everything seemed to be happening in slow motion. Sue saw a moment of ecstasy on Neville's face as the solid brass made contact with Sue's attacker, obliterated at once by creeping horror as he realized he had not hit the tattooed man hard enough to stop him.

But at least the man loosened his grip on Sue. She rolled away and jumped to her feet.

The tattooed man got up, staggered forward, then turned on Neville with a roar of fury.

Sue ran into the sitting-room to the phone. Before she had even thought what she was doing, she dialled Dugdale's direct line.

'Help,' she yelled down the line, 'you've got to help. He's going to kill us.'

She dropped the receiver as the tattooed man, his huge patterned hands clamped round Neville's throat, backed her friend into the room. Neville was choking, she saw the whites of his eyes, and his face was almost blue.

All the fight went out of her. She started to shake.

'Let him go,' she begged, 'please, let him go.'

She was clinging to a multi-coloured arm, trying to haul the man away from Neville, but he didn't seem even to notice her.

'If you want me to let 'im go, you tell me where Big Saul's money is and I'll think about it,' the tattooed man said.

'I don't know anything about Big Saul's money. Who is Big Saul, anyway?'

Sue could hear her voice sounding as terrified as she felt.

'You're makin' this a lot worse for your friend,' the tattooed man said, jerking Neville like a housewife shaking a pillow.

'I'll get money,' Sue said. 'I've got some money in the bank, you can have that. Just let him go before you kill him.'

'You're wasting my time,' the tattooed man said.

Neville's heels beat against the carpet; his hands, trying to prize open the tattooed man's grip on his throat, dropped to his sides and his body dangled limply from the grasp of the colourful fists.

'He's dead,' Sue said in a shaking voice, 'you've killed him, you bastard.'

The tattooed man seemed to toss Neville away in disgust.

Neville lay in a heap, like a remnant of one of his own rich fabrics thrown on the carpet.

Sue started to cry.

'Oh, God, Neville, I'm so sorry,' she whispered, leaning across to touch his face.

The tattooed man seemed a little disconcerted at what he had done.

'He asked for it,' he said. 'He hit me first.'

He looked at his grotesque great hands as though he had no connection with them and was surprised at what they had done. Then he saw the telephone receiver hanging free. He picked it up and said, 'Who's there? Is there anyone there?'

He listened for a moment, then crashed the receiver back on its rest.

'You fuckin' bitch, you called the police, didn't you? You've called the bloody cops.'

Sue tried to keep calm. She took a deep breath before she dared speak to him.

'Yes,' she said, 'they're on their way. You haven't time to kill me and get away, do you hear me?'

'I've time to stop your bleeding mouth for good and all,' he growled.

She backed away as he moved towards her, his arms outstretched to trap her.

He grabbed for her, but she ducked under his elbow and ran for the front door. She flung it open and rushed out, cannoning into the first of a line of uniformed policemen about to storm the flat.

They pushed her out of the way and rushed into the hallway together.

Sue found she couldn't move. She had fallen against the wall and knelt there shaking; she was clinging to the wall with its floral wallpaper as though for protection.

Then someone touched her shoulder and she looked up to see Dugdale and Malone looking down at her in concern. She couldn't read Dugdale's expression, but there was no mistaking the look on Sergeant Malone's face. He looked relieved.

25 Conduct Unbecoming

L ucy was working at the computer in Quentin Burns's office when Dugdale rang.

'What are you doing later?' he asked.

Lucy felt her mood lift. She had been depressed for days now, not sure what she was going to do next. Quentin and Tara had tried not to make her feel there was any pressure on her to find somewhere else to live, but she was very aware that she was in the way. The Burnses were trying to hold their marriage together and Tara did need someone who would listen while she poured her heart out. Normally, she would have come to Lucy; they'd have got a bit pissed, Tara would have grumbled about Quentin, invited Lucy's advice, and come to some kind of resolution by rejecting that advice on the basis that Lucy was old-fashioned, unmarried, and out of touch.

But that tried and true system was impossible now with Lucy in some kind of wounded emotional state, a guest in the conjugal home. Tara had no idea how to approach Lucy anyway, not now she was devastated by the way her settled life had suddenly fallen apart with Paul's death and deceit. Lucy, who would have helped if she could, knew that Tara's present rather feverish insouciance about her relationship with Quentin was a façade put on to make Lucy herself feel at ease.

In those moments when Lucy felt most guilty about being an imposition on her friends, she sometimes wondered why Tara couldn't unburden herself to Maxine instead, particularly when she must know that Lucy herself needed someone to talk to. But then, she thought, I couldn't have a heart to heart about things to Max either, she wouldn't understand. Max was far too sensible to have much sympathy for Lucy's all too feminine dithering.

And all the time Quentin used Lucy's stay as a way of distancing himself from the disintegrating lives of both his wife and Lucy. This wasn't particularly deliberate; Quentin simply thought that they could be of more help to each other than he could be to either. His one concession to taking action was to look up the menopause on the internet, but he decided that both Tara and Lucy were too young to be affected by it.

In any case, neither Tara nor Lucy could ever have confided in him about emotional matters.

Lucy wasn't sure why this was. Quentin was a good friend. He had made practical suggestions to Lucy about her immediate future. Lucy supposed that Tara and Quentin had once been able to talk on that level, but the problems in their marriage, whatever they were, had driven them apart. She didn't know why it seemed out of the question for her to confide in Quentin about her own feelings because sometimes, when they were working together, she felt a strong desire to do so. But the fact that Quentin was married to her friend seemed to put any such intimacy out of bounds, however innocent.

But Guy Dugdale was different. Hearing his voice on the phone, Lucy imagined those deep dark eyes fixed on hers, full of understanding; she felt that she could tell him anything.

Except that I love him, Lucy told herself, I can't tell him that because I'm not sure how he feels about me. And anyway, she thought, he'd run a mile if I did make a declaration of passion, and, yes, she knew that should have told her something if she was prepared to listen. Which she wasn't, not yet.

On the phone to Guy, she sounded a little breathless as she said, 'I'm working at the moment, finishing off a load of letters that've built up over the last ten days. But I'll be through them by three or four.'

'Good,' he said, 'I'm coming down to see you. There's something we have to clear up about Paul's death.'

His matter-of-fact tone jerked her out of her fantasizing.

'You can come here,' she said, giving him the Burnses' address. 'My friends won't be back till later.' Then she added, 'It's weird not having a home of my own any more.'

And I can't ask him to spend the night, she thought. We can't even go to my bedroom for an hour or so because it would be rude to do it in their house.

It seemed to her that Dugdale knew what she was thinking.

'Depending on when I get down,' he said, 'I'll put up at the local pub. Perhaps we could eat there, the two of us?' he said.

'That would be great,' she said. 'It's called *The Cross Keys*. I'll see you when you get here, then.'

He could hear how much the invitation cheered her.

Malone's right, he thought, I'll have to tread carefully there. Neither of these two women is quite normal. Surely, he said to himself, it can't be normal for young women who've just lost their two-timing boyfriend in messy circumstances to throw themselves at the unfortunate cop who's trying to sort out his murder. Were they clinging to him as some sort of father figure? Surely not, he thought, they're not children. But if it's not that, what the hell is it?

And then he asked himself. Is it normal, what I'm doing? All this nonsense may have started because I wanted to help them, but I'm a policeman heading an investigation and I'm way out of line.

Then he told himself, I'm doing what I have to do to get to the bottom of this case. There's nothing in the book to say I can't enjoy myself in the process. And what's wrong with making two unhappy women feel a bit better while I'm investigating?

Dugdale was glad that Malone wasn't there to hear what was

going on in his head. Derek had a nasty knack of knowing. He could imagine exactly what the sergeant would say in one of his deafening muttered sarcasms.

In spite of himself, he was looking forward to seeing Lucy again. The sound of her voice still gave him a peculiar urge to take care of her, and let her take care of him. He had to talk to her anyway. He had to ask her about the phone call Sue Stockland had talked about; the call from Lucy warning Sue about the tattooed man, the one which Neville had answered.

That was in the line of work. But he could easily have asked that on the phone.

He was going down to the country for much more than that; or, at least, he hoped he was.

The question is, he asked himself, would I be going to see her if the tattooed man hadn't actually attacked Sue and killed Neville?

Who cares? he thought, I don't have to make a choice one way or another.

Meanwhile Lucy, knowing nothing about Neville's murder, was excited that this man, as handsome as a film star, was driving two hundred miles simply to spend the evening with her.

And possibly the night, she told herself, trying hard to concentrate on Quentin's letter to a local hotelier about a website design for his business; possibly the whole night.

Would Tara and Quentin be offended, she wondered, if she disappeared to the pub to meet someone for dinner and didn't get back to their house until the next day?

So what if they are, Lucy thought, I want to be with him tonight more than anything in the world. And they need to have the place to themselves for a while.

When she had finished the letters Quentin had left for her, Lucy went to her room and spent nearly two hours getting ready for Guy's visit.

Then she sat on the bed and waited.

She was reminded of all those Friday nights waiting for Paul. But it's not the same, she thought. She was waiting in excited anticipation for Guy Dugdale, but also she was waiting in some trepidation for either Tara or Quentin to come home. She tried to remember the thrilling angst in the old days before Paul was killed, the waiting painful but something excitingly private between them. Those long, agonizing evenings were as nothing to what she was going through now. It was one thing longing for the arrival of the object of desire; what was much more intensely painful now was hoping that the Burnses wouldn't get home before he came. If they did, she'd have to introduce them. She would probably have to ask them to come to the pub. I don't want to share him, she said to herself, praying to some indiscriminate fate, please, please, don't let me have to share him.

Dugdale rang her just as Lucy saw the headlights of a car turn into the drive. He was running late, he said, he would meet her at the pub, was that OK?

'Yes, yes, goodbye,' she said, and put the phone down before he could say anything else.

She heard the car draw up outside. Either Tara or Quentin was coming home.

Lucy grabbed her handbag and ran through the kitchen out of the back door. As it closed behind her, she heard Tara call her name from the front hall.

Then Maxine's voice said, 'She's not here.'

'Thank God,' Tara said, 'poor Lucy, I'm sorry for her, but I'm beginning to feel it's not my house any more.'

I've got to find a place of my own, Lucy thought, I need somewhere I can call home. There was that cottage in the village for sale, the one near her father's old church. I'll go and look at it on Monday, she told herself.

She walked round the side of the house to the drive. It was raining, not hard, but that soft persistent drizzle that played havoc with her thick, wiry hair. What was Guy going to think when he saw her looking like a wild woman? She would have to walk to *The Cross Keys*, too, because her car was parked in the Burnses' drive and it was of an age when it only started under noisy protest. Tara would be bound to hear her.

Looking from the shrubbery through the window into the lighted front room of the house, Lucy could see Tara wandering round turning on the table lamps. Maxine was on her knees in front of the dead fire, twisting the pages of a newspaper to light it. Tara turned off the central light. The room looked comfortable, friendly. Tara went to the side table where they kept the drinks and poured herself a vodka and tonic. She looked at Maxine and appeared to be asking her what she wanted to drink. For a moment, Lucy envied them; they looked so unthreatened by the outside world. She wished that she could watch Tara and Quentin together without them knowing she was there. From what Tara had told her, and from studying the way they treated each other in company, with a kind of mocking indifference, Lucy knew all she wanted to know about the troubled public face of their marriage. But what were they like when they were alone? Did they bicker? Or did they sit in front of the television in glum silence? Lucy was curious. She didn't really understand how other women behaved in their relationships with men.

Lucy had been asking herself questions about this since she'd learned about Sue Stockland's relationship with Paul. It seemed to Lucy that Sue had created an emotional bond with Paul which was utterly different from the way it had been between Paul and herself. Not only different, Lucy thought, but better. Sue and Paul were more like equals, while Lucy saw herself as something between a little sister and an eighteenth-century parlour maid out of a Fielding novel. It seemed to her that loving Paul had been a kind of initiation process, and now, with Guy Dugdale, she was ready to fly.

Dugdale was in the bar of *The Cross Keys* when Lucy got there. He saw her in the doorway, her pale hair wild and wonderful, sparkling with raindrops like diamonds under the light. Her damp dress clung to her, showing her in outline like a Greek statue, naked, luxuriant, and seductive.

She seemed to Dugdale like a vision of the essential feminine. He was disarmed.

'Come up to my room,' he said. 'You need to get dry.'

He found he could hardly speak, he wanted so urgently to be alone with her. As he followed her up the stairs to his room, he imagined he heard Malone's disapproving warning in his ear, and he laughed out loud. To hell with you, Sergeant, he thought.

Lucy, misinterpreting his laughter, looked back at him from the landing.

'I didn't do it deliberately,' she said. 'Get wet, I mean.' She floundered for an explanation. 'The car wouldn't start,' she said.

He moved past her to open the door to his room. As he fiddled with the key, he could feel her pressing against him. She seemed to be burning. He stood aside to let her into the room and followed her in, locking the door behind him.

Thank God, there wasn't anything coy about her. He wondered if he should ask his questions first, but he saw her peel off the wet dress and stand naked in front of him, her body glowing pink with damp. Lucy certainly wasn't coy. Dugdale was overawed. When he took her in his arms, he was afraid that he would weep.

An hour later, with a strong wind driving the rain against the small uncurtained window of the bedroom in the old pub, Lucy said, 'What did you want to ask me? You know, about Paul?'

Dugdale, half asleep, tried to remember what other reason he could have had for coming here but to make love to Lucy.

'Paul?' he said. 'Oh, yes.'

He roused himself and started to dress.

Lucy watched him, trying not to laugh.

'Do you have to be dressed to ask me official questions?' she said. 'I'm surprised you haven't brought Sergeant Malone along to write down what I say and use it in evidence against me.'

Dugdale looked embarrassed.

'I'm sorry,' he said, 'it's just that I can't get my head round work being a pleasure like this.'

Fully dressed, he sat down on the side of the bed looking down at her.

'Why did you ring Sue Stockland warning her about Jed Mallet being out to get her?'

'Is that his name, the tattooed man? I rang her because he came here and threatened me. He was looking for money that he said Paul owed to a man called Big Saul. He wanted to know where Paul had hidden it, and I was so scared I told him it might be wherever Paul lived with Sue Stockland.'

She saw Dugdale draw away from her and thought he was blaming her.

Quickly she said, 'I know it was a terrible thing to do, but I thought he'd kill me. I said the first thing to come into my head to get rid of him. And then he went and I realized what I'd done and I tried to get in touch with her to warn her. But all I could do was leave a message with a man who answered the phone, who sounded as though he wasn't quite right in the head. Sue wasn't there. Oh, God, has something happened to her?'

Dugdale wasn't sure what to tell Lucy now. If he told her that the tattooed man had murdered Neville in Sue's flat, it was bound to ruin the rest of his visit. She'd think it was her fault. He told himself that Lucy didn't need to know, not yet, anyway. There was nothing she could add. Jed Mallet was in custody, there was no need of a description of him from Lucy.

Lucy should know, though, that the man who had threatened her had been caught. She had to know that, and if he told her that, he would have to tell her where he had been caught and why.

My poor Lucy, he thought.

'Sue's fine,' he said. 'But the tattooed man did go to the flat.' Dugdale hesitated, then went on in a flat voice as though he was giving evidence in court. 'He killed the man you talked to on the phone. Neville Smith, his name was. He was quite a well-known dress designer, also an ex-junkie, according to Sue. He put up a fight, but he was never a match for a thug like Mallet.'

Lucy sat up in the bed, appalled.

'But Guy, it was my fault. If I'd never mentioned that Paul lived with her …'

'Why didn't you tell the police about that man coming here and scaring you?'

Lucy frowned. 'I don't know,' she said. 'I thought I was being hysterical about the whole thing. Nothing really happened except this thug came and asked where Paul might have left his money. I didn't want the police nosing into Paul's financial affairs because I made a real fool of myself selling up to give him the money.' She lay down again. 'Honestly, Guy, I don't know. I just thought I'd over-reacted. If I had reported it, would it have saved Neville's life?'

Dugdale took her hand. 'I doubt it,' he said. 'By the time the local cops had got around to mentioning it to us, if they ever did, it would've been far too late to stop anything. Luckily Sue was able to get a call to us and we've got that tattooed bastard bang to rights for murder, and we're well on the way to putting Big Saul behind bars, which is something we've been trying to do for years.'

'Oh,' Lucy said, 'that's all right, then. There's nothing like looking on the bright side, I suppose, but however you look at it, that poor Neville person is dead.'

'We're pretty sure that Mallet killed Paul, too,' he said. 'Malone's working on him to get enough evidence for a conviction.'

Lucy looked at him quickly, hearing a note of doubt in his

voice. 'You're not sure, are you?' she said. 'You don't think he killed Paul?'

'Oh, he's a murderer, no doubt of that. I practically saw him kill Neville with my own eyes. But Meyer? Malone is convinced and he says he's got the evidence to charge Mallet, but no, you're quite right, my instinct tells me that that one's down to someone else.'

'And that someone else could be me?' Lucy said. 'Aren't I one of the usual suspects?'

'Yes,' Guy said, 'I suppose you are.'

26 The Merry Widow

Dugdale drove back to London before dawn the next morning. He was early enough to miss the weekday build-up of traffic on the M5 around Bristol, and had a clear run through on the M4 until he reached Slough. It took him longer to reach central London from there than the rest of his journey put together.

He'd intended to turn right off the Marylebone Road down Gloucester Place, but it was as though the car refused to obey him. He even found that he had manoeuvred himself into the inner lane, among the heavy lorries and buses.

What am I thinking of? he asked himself. It was as though he was operating on automatic pilot.

Half an hour later he was parked on a meter behind Euston Station and marching across Eversholt Street to the grim little hotel where Vita Meyer had booked in off the train from Manchester.

There was still a sign in the window advertising vacancies. The narrow hall and the cramped reception desk under the stairs showed no more sign of human habitation than it had when he and Malone had been here before. This time, though, there was a damp odour of frying hovering on the narrow stairs as Dugdale made his way up to Vita's room.

If she was surprised to see him, she showed no sign of it. She was already dressed, which surprised him. The Vita he remembered from the old days in Manchester was a creature of the night. Then it occurred to him that perhaps he was so early she hadn't gone to bed yet.

She smiled at him and laughed.

'Don't tell me you've come for breakfast,' she said. 'You'd be much better off in the police canteen.'

'I believe you,' he said. 'Thank God, I'm not that desperate.'

'We've got our own kettles in the rooms,' she said, turning away from the door. 'So I can make you coffee.'

He followed her into the room. The bed had evidently been slept in. Vita must have changed her nocturnal ways, he thought.

She filled the kettle at the hand basin and started to tear sachets of instant coffee and sugar into the two cups.

'There's powdered cream or everlasting milk in whatever they call those horrible little cartons I can never open without squirting the stuff all over my clothes. Take your pick.'

Dugdale nudged a pile of underwear off the only chair in the room and sat down. It was that or the edge of the unmade bed, where he thought he would be at a disadvantage if Vita sat next to him.

'Tetrapaks,' he said, 'that's what they call them. Black, please.'

The kettle boiled. Vita filled the cups and handed one to him. She put hers on the bedside table and jumped on to the bed, pulling the bedclothes over her legs and leaning back against the pillows.

'Now,' she said, smiling again, 'don't tell me this is a social visit. What do you want from me?' She tilted her head and pouted at him.

For one horrible moment, Dugdale thought she was coming on to him. 'No, no.' he said hastily, before realizing that of course Vita had no ulterior motive. She was simply mocking him.

He felt his neck go red with embarrassment. But how could she know what I was thinking? he thought, she's just doing what comes naturally.

She seemed extraordinarily good-humoured. Positively the merry widow.

He said, 'Actually, I was passing, and there are one or two things I wanted to check.' He knew that he sounded flustered and smiled at her. 'I'm sorry,' he said, 'I never thought I'd hear myself saying that in earnest ... "I was just passing" ... but it happens to be true.'

'If that's your usual line with the girls, Inspector, I'll bet your sex life isn't nearly as good as it could be,' Vita said, teasing him.

'Oh, hell,' Dugdale said, 'that's not what I meant and you know it.'

But she's taken the initiative, he thought, she's making fun of me.

'This coffee's disgusting,' he said.

'I put whisky in mine. It's better that way. But you're on duty?'

'Yes,' he said. He felt that he'd scored a tiny victory by not falling into the trap he imagined she'd set for him. 'Yes, I am on duty. There are still some questions, I'm afraid....'

'I thought it would be cut and dried by now,' she said. 'You've got the man who did it, haven't you?'

'We haven't charged anyone yet. What makes you think it's all over?' he asked.

'That tattooed man? The one who attacked that flashy tart who said she was Paul's girlfriend and then killed the man who was with her. You arrested him. I read about it in the paper.'

'Why should you think he had anything to do with Paul's death?'

'The paper said he'd gone to the flat to get some money Paul owed him. Isn't that right?'

Dugdale looked at her. Had the papers speculated like that? He wasn't sure. He shrugged. 'There are still unanswered questions,' he said.

'Like what?' she asked, and her sharp tone was at odds with

her languorous pose on the bed and the rather flirtatious smile she gave him.

He was silent and she went on: 'Sorry, Inspector, I wasn't trying to be rude, but the sooner we can sort out about what happened to Paul, the sooner I can get all the legal stuff under way and get on with my life. As it is, everything seems to be on hold. After all, there's no real reason to think Paul was even murdered, is there? It could easily have been suicide, or an accident.'

'Oh,' Dugdale said, 'I don't think there's much chance of that.'

'But why not? Why don't you? Don't people like you ever think how all these complications you create cause terrible problems for the families? How can you be so sure?'

Dugdale looked at her, sprawling on the bed like that, and sounding so sincere.

'Oh,' he said, 'the wheels of justice and all that, they grind slowly but they grind exceedingly small.'

'Bollocks,' she said, and laughed at him. 'It cuts both ways, Mr Policeman. I understand you need evidence to make your charges stick, but surely when you get a case like Paul's where apparently you haven't got any evidence at all that he was murdered, even, you shouldn't hold things up for the real life people involved because you'd rather have a nice juicy murder case to solve than a boring suicide or a routine accidental overdose.'

Dugdale thought back to that early morning when he and Malone had been called to the Soho alley where Paul Meyer's body had been found. He'd been annoyed, he remembered that, having to deal with a routine case. He'd been bored, too, at the thought of yet another drugs-related death, another fatal overdose. The question of murder hadn't occurred to him until he recognized Meyer's dead face.

He didn't think that if he told Vita about that, she'd accept it as any kind of satisfactory evidence. So he ignored her comment and asked her, 'Tell me, why did you come to London when you heard he was alive? If you'd wanted money, you'd have been better to telephone. You might've known he'd have complications after all those years without you. In which case, he'd have paid to keep you away, wouldn't he?'

'Complications? Oh, you mean other women? Yes, you're probably right. But then, you see, that wasn't why I wanted to see him. It wasn't the money.'

'But your Manchester club's going bankrupt. You must've wanted money.'

'Oh, I did. But that doesn't mean I thought Paul could give it to me.'

'But Sue Stockland told you he was rich. You thought you could get him to clear your debts, you must've done.'

She gave him the sort of indulgent smile a glamorous grandmother might give to the innocent who tried to teach her to suck eggs.

'Do you imagine I'm going to believe what silly drunken little tarts tell me over a late-night bottle about the boyfriends who've stood them up? They're not going to say they've been dumped by no-marks without two pennies to rub together. That would make them look even more pathetic than they already do. They all say their boyfriends are rich and famous and good-looking.'

'And you thought Sue Stockland was one of those?'

'Of course she was one of those. What else would she be? She might be a hotshot business woman to you, but I know better. Underneath that glossy appearance, she's a woman scorned. I knew that the minute I saw her. At least she wasn't lying when she showed me a photo of Paul to prove he was beautiful. Even so, it was an old picture that must've been taken when they first met. He looked a lot older and not all that lovely when I identified him in the mortuary. But anyway, I knew Paul. I knew he could never be rich.'

'So why did you want to see him?' Dugdale asked. 'Don't tell me it was for old times' sake.'

Vita smiled again, but this time it was through the nostalgic film of once starry eyes.

'So there's a soft centre inside that tough policeman exterior,' Vita said. Then she suddenly dropped the teasing tone, and looked him straight in the eye. 'We were a good team, Paul and me, in the old days. I wanted us to get back together,' she said. 'I wanted for me to be his wife and for him to be my husband, for us to be a proper couple. I was still in love with him.' And the defiant look on her face dared Dugdale to call her a liar.

27 Down Memory Lane

'How are you?' Lucy asked Sue Stockdale.

It was because of Neville she was ringing, she told herself, she had to say something to Sue about Neville.

'Busy,' Sue said. Then she added, 'I mean there's plenty going on in the business, which keeps my mind off things. I didn't mean you're interrupting.'

'But I am?' Lucy said, joking.

Sue laughed. 'It's just something to say, isn't it? I'm glad to hear from you. How's the big romance?'

Lucy tried to remember what she'd told Sue about her relationship with Guy Dugdale. She was surprised that she'd revealed something so personal to someone she'd never actually met, but it wasn't as though Sue really was a stranger; in a way Lucy felt there was a closer bond between the two of them than she had with any other woman.

She hadn't mentioned Guy's name, she was sure of that. She hadn't wanted Sue to know that her new prospect was Guy, because of course Sue knew him. He'd questioned her about Paul and about the tattooed man who'd killed Neville.

Lucy was about to launch into enthusiastic detail, but then she thought, This call isn't about me.

'I really rang about your friend,' she said. 'I'm so sorry about what happened. I think it may've been my fault that brute of a man knew where to find you. He came down here and attacked me. He was trying to kill me and I was so scared I blurted out that Paul lived with you just to get rid of him. I didn't mean any harm, he was choking me and I was terrified.'

'I'd have done the same,' Sue said, 'I don't blame you for that.'

It was probably nothing, Lucy thought, Sue probably didn't mean anything by that. She can't blame me for Paul's death. And then she said to herself, I blamed her. I told Guy she killed him.

It was best to have this out, Lucy thought. She asked, 'Do you blame me for Paul? His death, I mean?'

To Lucy's surprise, Sue laughed. 'Not now. I did think you killed him,' she said, 'I told the police about you.'

She waited for Lucy to protest, or at least react. But Lucy said nothing, and there was something about the nature of the silence over the telephone line that made Sue suspicious.

'You knew, didn't you? How did you know that? You did know, didn't you?'

Lucy seemed to be trying not to laugh. 'I told them you did it,' she said. 'I suppose I expected you to do the same. It's funny, really, except I suppose it isn't really. I don't even know now what made me think you could've done it. Shock, I suppose, and finding out how he was two-timing us. I'm sorry.'

'Me, too. Funny how we both did the same thing. I wonder what the cops made of it?'

'Perhaps it happens a lot,' Lucy said. 'They can't have taken it very seriously, can they? If they had they'd be trying to charge us with wasting police time.'

'At least they've got that tattooed thug locked away. Even if they can't prove he killed Paul, they practically watched him kill Neville.'

Does she mean that? Lucy asked herself, does she blame Guy for failing Paul in some way? Lucy felt suddenly sorry for Sue, she sounded so bitter. And she had lost two people close to her. Being busy at work wouldn't make up for such a gap in her life.

'You're having a really bad time, aren't you?' Lucy said.

There was a pause, then Sue said, 'yes', and it sounded to Lucy as though she was trying not to cry.

Then quickly, as though she wanted to stop Lucy from trying to comfort her, Sue said, 'Lucy, do you care who killed Paul any more? Now he's dead, does it make any difference?'

Lucy was startled. She started to say something vague about wanting the murderer to pay for what he'd done, but then she stopped herself. It wasn't that simple. There was something behind Sue's question. Did she think Paul deserved what happened to him?

'I don't know,' she said. 'Honestly, I cared like hell at first but that could've been because I thought you'd done it and I wanted you to pay.'

'But don't you think you wanted me to pay because you'd found out about Paul and me, not because he'd been killed? That's how I felt, too, and that's what I wanted to make you pay for.'

'You know, I hadn't realized, but that's true,' Lucy said slowly, 'now I know the murderer was that awful man, it seems kind of impersonal, as though Paul's actual murder doesn't have much to do with me. He's dead and that's what matters, not the details of how he died. Is that weird?'

'Probably, but natural, too, I suppose,' Sue said. 'At least that's how it seems to me too, and I always think that what seems natural to me is natural, full stop. I feel worse about Neville. I blame myself for that. He wouldn't even have been in my flat if he hadn't been trying to help me.'

'Well there you are, hang on to that,' Lucy said, 'he wouldn't have been helping you if he hadn't wanted to, would he? So you can't blame yourself. He had a choice.'

'You've got quite a hard streak, haven't you?' Sue said, not without admiration. 'I'd never've guessed that about you.'

'I was just trying to make you feel better,' Lucy said. She was a little shocked that trying to look on the bright side could make her seem hard. Funny, she thought, Dad used to get irritated with me for trying to see the best in everything awful that happened. I've always done that, but then it was about blocked drains or another floor falling in; now it's about love and death and still someone can think I'm hard. But then she told herself, before Paul's death I'd never have had a conversation with anyone like Sue Stockland.

28 Another Dodgy Romance

Malone was already at his desk when Dugdale got to work. But of course he's been there for hours, his boss thought, it's mid-morning by now. He probably thinks I've only just started, he told himself, he thinks I'm late.

Dugdale didn't exactly resent that, but he wanted to put his sergeant right. Except Malone was laughing with a group of colleagues over the coffee machine and Dugdale felt bad about that. He knew that his sergeant was feeling particularly good because they'd had a result: two murders sorted and, thanks to some not-so-subtle psychological pressure on Jed Mallet, a promising, provable case against Big Saul, a known criminal who'd evaded justice for years.

Dugdale felt bad because he realized only too well how good Malone must feel and now he had to spoil things for him.

He called the sergeant into his office.

'Good morning, sir,' Malone said. He was clearly looking forward to the next case, hoping Dugdale was going to tell him what it would be. 'That was a good result in the Paul Meyer case, wasn't it?' he said. 'We've charged Jed Mallet with Neville's murder, of course. He's singing like a canary about Saul Kramer, too, hoping if he coughs up enough to put Big Saul inside, they'll go easier on him when he comes to court. He says killing Neville was an accident. He claims he was protecting himself when Neville attacked him.'

'Have you charged Mallet with Paul Meyer's murder yet?'

'No, sir, not until we've got as much as we can from him about Big Saul. And he's spinning us a yarn about that purple Lotus of Meyer's; and I thought I'd get someone to check that out before you have a go at him.'

'What's he saying?' Dugdale asked.

'He claims Meyer gave him the car in exchange for laying off collecting Big Saul's money for a few hours. Mallet's saying he took the keys but left the car where it was outside Meyer's office while he went off and had a few drinks. He says it's impossible to find a parking space round there at night.'

'Not much of an alibi so far, is it? Then what?'

'When he came back just before dawn he drove the car to Big Saul's place and had a bit of a look at his new possession. He found Meyer's body on the back seat. Still warm, according to him.'

'And?'

'He says he panicked, dumped the body there and drove away like a bat out of hell.'

'What did he do with the car?'

'He says he abandoned it in one of those streets off the Holloway Road and got a cab back to King's Cross to a snooker joint where he hung out for a few hours.

Dugdale didn't say anything to all of this. Malone, still flushed with victory, added:

'You wouldn't think he had the imagination to make up a story like that, would you, sir?

Dugdale leaned back in his chair and put his feet on his desk.

'I don't think he did it, Derek,' he said.

'You what?' Malone said, and added a rather startled 'sir.'

'I wish I didn't have to say this,' Dugdale said, 'but I don't think Jed Mallet killed Paul Meyer.'

'But it's an open-and-shut case. We can place him in Paul Meyer's office. There's forensic evidence and an eyewitness, the newspaper-seller. Sure, Big Saul was probably behind it and, to shift the blame, Mallet may give us the gen on that. But it's a sure thing Mallet did the actual killing. We can get him on it, no problem.'

'It's all circumstantial. No forensic.'

'There's a DNA link on the body; Mallet manhandled Meyer. We can prove that.'

'But nothing on the syringe.'

'Nothing at all. Only Meyer's prints. But then, you're so sure it was murder, not suicide or an accident. Aren't you, sir?'

'I know, Derek, I know you're right and we'd get a conviction on Mallet, no doubt about that at all,' Dugdale said, and then added, 'I know that bastard Mallet's a killer, and at least we've got him for the fashion designer fellow's murder anyway, so why not put him away and kill two birds with one stone? But I don't think he killed Meyer and I can't help it, I'm going to have to prove it.'

'Bloody lawyers,' Malone said, with no attempt to prevent Dugdale hearing him.

Dugdale laughed, but he also looked apologetic, which gave Malone pause. He thought for a moment. Then he sat down in the chair facing Dugdale across the desk.

'Why don't you think he's guilty?' he asked.

Dugdale swung his feet off the desk and leaned forward towards Malone.

'You see, that's another interesting difference between the legal and the police mind,' he said. 'I do think he's guilty. I know he is. I practically saw him kill Neville. But I think he's guilty in a general sense, not in this particular, and for you it's strictly on a case by case basis.'

'With respect, sir, you're not a lawyer now, you're a cop. You did a law degree but you didn't want to be a lawyer, isn't that right? You're a bloody detective chief inspector, so quite a lot of people along the line must've thought you were a good cop.'

'But you don't, do you?'

Malone realized he was treading on thin ice and hesitated. Then he plainly decided he might as well be hung for a sheep as a lamb.

'I don't think you've got a real policeman's way of going about our work,' Malone said, trying to choose his words carefully. He sounded grudging when he added, 'But that's not to say I don't think that your sort of approach doesn't have a part to play in getting it right. Sometimes, anyway. And so I'd like to know why you think Jed Mallet didn't kill Paul Meyer. I respect what you think, even if I don't agree, because if I'd said what I've just said to what I'd call a real detective chief inspector, I'd be up before a disciplinary hearing already.'

Dugdale smiled at him and Malone smiled back.

'Right,' Dugdale said, 'I think Mallet went to squeeze Saul Kramer's money out of Meyer. I think he may have intended to take the money and kill him. But Meyer hadn't got the money there. What I think our Paul did was convince Mallet that he'd have it by the end of the night, next morning, some time very soon, and Mallet agreed to give him time. Jed wouldn't have fancied the prospect of telling Big Saul he hadn't got the money, so he took a chance. Meyer probably bribed him to lay off for a few hours.'

'What with?' Malone asked. 'We know he hadn't any money.'

Dugdale considered. 'With the purple sports car, just as Mallet says. He fancied driving around Soho in that with the top down showing off his tattoos.'

'The mind boggles,' Malone said. 'He's not the right shape. If he ever managed to get into that car, I doubt he'd ever get out.'

'Quite,' Dugdale said, 'which is really the same reason I don't think he would have made Meyer's death look like a heroin overdose. It's just not his style. It's not as if he hasn't killed before and it's always been in some directly violent way – stabbing or clubbing or with guns. A man like that sticks to what's worked for him before. He doesn't suddenly branch out into clever phony overdoses.'

'The method could be down to Saul Kramer?' Malone suggested.

'True, but why should Kramer interfere in this case? Mallet's killed for Kramer before, he's told us that himself, and it's always been by the methods that come naturally to him. Meyer was beaten up, but three or four hours before he died. We can probably put that down to Mallet, so that explains the DNA you found on Meyer's body. But why would he go back and slip him some chemical knock-out drop and inject him with heroin? He'd simply hit him harder.'

'Yes,' Malone said, 'manual methods are cheaper.'

'There's that, too, but drugs and so on make it too complicated.'

Then Malone said, 'Let's say you're right, then the question is, "Who did do it?" Which brings us straight back to your lady friends.'

They both sat for several minutes facing each other in silence and thinking their own thoughts.

'I went to see Vita this morning on my way in,' Dugdale said at last.

'You were just passing and....'

'Shut up,' Dugdale said. 'She confided in me. She told me the real reason she came to London to see him. She was still in love with him, she wanted them to get back together. It wasn't the money. She knew he wasn't rich.'

For a brief moment, before Dugdale finished his sentence, Malone's face softened and he looked almost sentimental. But by the time Dugdale said 'It wasn't the money', Malone's expression had returned to normal cynicism.

'Pull the other one,' Malone said.

'I know. But who's to say it isn't true? If she sticks to that story, bang goes her motive. There'd be no reason for her to kill him if she knew he wasn't rich and she had no expectations of an inheritance. And she's bloody convincing. I might've believed her myself if I didn't know better.'

'You might as well face it, we've no real case against her,' Malone said. He made no effort to hide his opinion that his boss was failing in professional detachment in this investigation.

Dugdale acknowledged Malone's view. He knew he wasn't being logical.

'And yet I'd put my pension on it,' he said, 'Vita Meyer did it.'

'But?'

'We can't prove it? I know, but if you can suspend your inner policeman for a moment, I think I know how we might force her hand and get the proof we need.'

29 Dugdale and Sue

Malone had said not long ago that Dugdale had a way with women, but only one way.

Dugdale thought of that remark as he lay sprawled on Sue Stockland's bed with Sue's head against his shoulder and her soft hair draped across his face. He'd overheard Malone say it when he was talking to someone else and Dugdale thought it funny. But was it intended as a joke, he wondered, or as a reproof?

He felt Sue's lips against his ear, and then her tongue.

My God, he thought, what does bloody Malone do in circumstances like these? Derek's not a bad-looking guy, he might be quite attractive to women, this kind of thing must've happened to him. Does he simply tell them he's a married man and that's all it takes?

But Dugdale had tried that and it hadn't made any difference. Paul Meyer had claimed to have children, as well as being married, and that hadn't put Lucy or Sue off him.

But Meyer had been clever, Dugdale thought, he'd tailored the imaginary wife and kids he'd pretended to have to exploit the sort of women Lucy and Sue were. He'd played on their particular fears and weaknesses about themselves to the point that they were glad to hold off on a full relationship with him. He convinced both of them that there was a limit to what he had to offer without either one of them suspecting for a moment that he didn't love her. They sympathized that he could go so far and no further. So the stereotypical, wannabe wife and earth-mother, Lucy, forgave Paul everything because of his handicapped daughter; and Sue, who would have worked her fingers to the bone to send any child of hers to boarding school as soon as legally possible, could put marriage on ice because Paul's invented problem-sons constituted her worst nightmare.

He must've been a cold-hearted bastard, Dugdale thought. He exploited those poor women's basic natures and played them off against themselves. I don't think I could do that, however desperate I was.

Dugdale brought his mind back to Malone and the way he avoided complications with women. He decided that there must be something about the way Derek said he was already taken, something that made these women believe it. That must be what made the difference. I haven't got the knack yet, Dugdale told himself. It must be something to do with the fact that Malone really wasn't interested in any woman except his wife. He didn't have to tell women that, somehow they knew it. Just as, whatever he said himself, they knew that he was up for it, he wanted what happened. Dugdale was interested in all women as long as they weren't really his wife.

'Hey, stop that, don't you know I'm a married man,' he told Sue, but, listening to himself, he could tell he didn't sound convincing.

'Look,' he said, 'I came to ask for your help.'

She raised her head to look down at his face. 'So this was part of a softening up process? Shame on you, taking advantage of a poor girl.'

'Yes,' Dugdale said, 'you could say that.'

The detective chief inspector didn't have much of a sense of humour.

She laughed and rolled away from him. 'Get dressed,' she said. 'I've got the feeling this is going to be something we need to discuss with our clothes on.'

She picked up her scattered underwear and went to the bathroom. She had a wonderful backside, Dugdale thought, watching her walk away.

He almost caught her arm to pull her back on to the bed. But he had to talk seriously to her.

He began to put on his clothes.

'I saw Ted on my way up,' he said, making conversation while he considered how to say what he wanted from her. 'When did he get back to work?'

Sue raised her voice above the sound of running taps to answer. 'Yesterday, I think,' she said. 'He's a bit battered, but OK. Actually, I've got a theory he wanted to get back to work before his battle scars faded. He's becoming a bit of an Ancient Mariner about it. I suppose it brings in the tips.'

She's a hard-nosed bitch, Dugdale thought, but it made him smile.

He'd been dressed for some time before she emerged from the bathroom. She looked, he said to himself, as though she was about to conduct a business meeting.

'Right,' she said. 'Now what do you want me to do?'

He was disconcerted that she was so direct. He'd taken it for granted that she thought he would want to talk about their relationship.

'It's about Paul's murder,' he said.

She looked surprised. 'But isn't that sorted. I thought you'd got that tattooed freak for both killings, Paul's and Neville's?'

'I don't think Jed Mallet killed Paul.'

Sue looked horrified. 'Don't be ridiculous,' she said. 'Of course he did.' She looked at him with a sly expression. 'Unless, of course, you've come round to my way of thinking,' she said, 'and think it was Lucy Drake.'

'No,' he said, 'not Lucy. At least I don't think it was Lucy.'

'Well it wasn't me,' she said, 'so if it wasn't the Upholstered Man, who was it?'

'I think it was Vita.'

Sue's eyes narrowed. 'The wife, Vita…. Why?'

'I think she'd forgotten all about Paul Meyer till you walked into that bankrupt club of hers and gave her the impression that her ex was rich as Croesus.'

'Who's Croesus?'

'Greece's version of Donald Trump. You told her Paul was rich, and then she suddenly remembered she was married to him and as his wife …'

'… she would inherit as next of kin.' Sue sat down on the bed. She looked thoughtful. 'Yes,' she said, 'she knew he'd never have thought of making a will. The bitch.' She turned to Dugdale. 'She'd get the money once he was dead. Is that all you've got to go on?'

'Well,' he said, aware that really, yes, it was all he had. 'There were refinements. I think she rang you and told you to ring Lucy because she thought one or both of you would be chief suspect.'

Thank God Malone isn't here taking notes, Dugdale thought, it's probably a gross infringement of the police code to turn a witness against a suspect by suggesting the suspect had planned to frame her for the crime.

Sue jumped to her feet. 'God, that cow! I'll make her pay for that.'

'It might've worked,' Dugdale said, 'all she had to do was kill him, establish herself as his legally wedded wife and make a show of discovering about his tragic, self-inflicted death. Actually, of course, so far it *has* worked.'

'Except he didn't have any money. I was lying to Vita.'

'Yes,' said Dugdale, 'she's thought of that. She's saying now that she knew you were lying about the money, but when you showed her Paul's picture it reminded her of her marriage vows, and she couldn't wait to return to the conjugal fold and get back together with her husband.'

'So that means if she knew he wasn't rich, she wouldn't have any motive for killing him because there was nothing to inherit, right?'

'You've got it in one. I hope you never turn to crime, you'd be a formidable crook.'

Sue laughed. 'I'd rather be a detective. Tell me, why are you so sure Paul was murdered?'

Dugdale tried to remember. 'Because I knew who he was from way back,' he said. 'Just that, really. And I was bored. It's not much to go on, is it?'

'It won't convince a jury, if that's what you mean.' Sue began to pace up and down the room thinking.

'You see,' Dugdale said, speaking slowly as though he wasn't sure how to make this point, 'if we can't prove it was Vita, and I can't believe it was the technicolour tattooed thug, we have to come back to you and Lucy as prime suspects.'

'But why should I kill Paul? I loved him.'

Remembering the sensation of her tongue in his ear, Dugdale almost blurted out that if she'd really loved Paul she had an odd way of showing it, but he stopped himself in time.

'Because you and Lucy found out about each other and how he'd betrayed you, which gave you both a reason to want to kill him.'

'Yes, well, I'd still put money on Lucy,' Sue said. 'If it was Vita, why would she kill him in an alley like that? She must've arranged to meet him. Why pick on a place like that for their reunion?'

'That's one of the things we've got to find out. But it's possible Mallet found Paul dead when he went to Paul's office to collect Big Saul's money, and he dumped the body in the alley because he knew that earlier on he'd left his fingerprints all over Meyer's office.'

'When you say that's one of the things we've got to find out,' Sue said, 'do you mean we, the police in general, or you and Sergeant Malone, or you and me?' Sue looked curious, not doubtful.

Dugdale would have liked to skirt round his plan before he broached it. He hadn't prepared for such a direct question. So he plunged straight ahead. 'You and Lucy Drake,' he said. 'Together, I thought you might help me prove the case against Vita.'

'How could we do that?'

Dugdale explained what he had in mind and half expected to be attacked.

But Sue Stockland started to laugh. 'My God,' she said, and there was a note of admiration in her voice, 'you must be off your head.' Then she added, 'Or desperate.'

30 The Two Women

'Can you believe we're doing this?' Sue said.

She and Lucy eyed each other. They were both thinking the same thing; each saw the other as Paul's woman on the side. They had unwittingly shared him, and during their telephone conversations had built up their own picture of the other. Now, face-to-face for the first time, they were trying to adjust their preconceptions to reality.

To Lucy, Sue Stockland was exactly the woman she had expected Paul to find attractive. Sue was beautiful, Lucy thought, she was sophisticated, fashionably dressed, well-groomed and sure of herself. Why had he even looked at me? she asked herself, staring at Sue to find any flaw at all. There didn't seem to be any – Lucy hadn't noticed the big feet.

Sue's first reaction to Lucy Drake was dismissive but unsurprised. She saw a big, frumpy country girl with split ends and wind-reddened cheeks which, if they weren't already, would soon be threaded by tiny red veins. Lucy was going to have to learn to use basic skin care and makeup if she wasn't going to look fifty by the time she was forty, Sue thought. She wondered if she should drop a hint. It wasn't altogether flattering to find that her rival for Paul's love was so nondescript. Lucy's clothes were colourless, shapeless, and looked home-made. Or is that her figure? Sue asked herself. She felt that Lucy could never compare with herself on any level, and she also felt that because of that she had triumphed over this other woman in Paul's life.

She wondered what Paul had expected to gain from an association with Lucy, but maybe it was the money he was after, much more money, apparently, than she herself was able to muster.

Whatever, Sue thought, Paul took her for a ride as well as me.

Dugdale had arranged for them to meet in the bar of a hotel off Sloane Square. On the phone, he'd told Lucy part of his theory that Paul had been murdered by his wife Vita and that he needed to confront Vita with his version before he could take action. He'd told her that he wanted her to collaborate with Sue to make this happen.

'It's a great excuse to get you up here, and when I get away from work, we can be together,' he'd said.

He knew he was being a rat, but he sensed that if he hadn't offered her that bait, she would refuse a straight request to take part.

'Please, Lucy, I can't wait to see you,' he'd said.

After that, nothing would have kept her away. Confronting Sue, the police investigation, even Vita as the prime suspect in Paul's murder, seemed incidental.

Also it never occurred to Lucy, an inveterate reader of Agatha Christie books on long winter evenings, to question Dugdale's professional methods. It seemed to her an acceptable way of establishing guilt of which Hercule Poirot or Miss Marple would have been proud.

But she was nervous of meeting Sue. She wondered if she should tell Guy that the two of them had talked quite often over the phone, but decided that she wanted to keep that between herself and Sue. And she thought, I'm looking forward to it, to the two of us meeting. And then she tried to put out of her mind the creeping fear that Sue would detect somehow that she and Guy were involved, and would try to steal him. Lucy couldn't help thinking that women like Sue couldn't control themselves.

'Of course I'll come,' she said, 'if you think it will help.'

'That's my girl,' Dugdale said.

Malone had listened to this conversation with Lucy, and when Dugdale put the receiver down, he looked disapproving.

Dugdale grinned at him. 'OK, I know, it's not procedure by the book,' he said, and added, 'I'll tell you one thing I've learned for nothing, though. Any future case involving a woman, my first rule will be to *cherchez les hormones*. I never had any idea they could have such an overwhelming effect on emotional females.'

'Welcome to the facts of life,' Malone said. 'Better late than never.' Then under his breath he muttered, 'Perhaps your Dad should have spent his money on a course in sexual diplomacy.'

'Money?' Dugdale asked, distracted. 'What's money got to do with it?'

'The money he gave you to take a tom up an alley in Soho,' Malone said.

'My God,' Dugdale said, 'how did you know about that?'

'I'm a cop,' Malone said. He saw that Dugdale didn't understand his attempt at a joke, so he added, 'Besides, you told me and I never forget what people tell me.'

Dugdale had nothing to say to that. He left the office. He was late for the meeting between Lucy Drake and Sue Stockland. He hadn't meant to be. He wanted to be there. As it was, the two women sat facing each other across a coffee table and continued to speculate about what Paul had seen in the other.

Lucy, watching Sue sip a bright blue cocktail, leaving the imprint of her lips like an advertisement on the glass, began to find a few flaws in the perfection. She began to feel sorry for Sue. She saw the hard edge to Sue's mouth and there were definitely frown lines under the perfect make-up, as well as something arrogant in the expression in her eyes. Lucy saw why Paul would turn from such a girl to a woman like herself.

And Sue, with a pang of envy, looked behind the stereotypical country bumpkin gulping a gin and tonic to see the laughter in Lucy's eyes, the generosity of her comfortable body, and an outgoing quality in her approach to life. She was his refuge, Sue thought, with her he could feel protected, safe enough to pretend to be himself. And she found herself thinking, I wish she was my friend.

This conceit struck her as funny. She smiled at her private joke and Lucy smiled back.

'Are you coping?' Sue asked.

'Sure I am. And I can see you are, you look great,' Lucy said.

They sat for a moment in silence, both thinking how weird it was to meet as a stranger someone they'd learned so much about. Both felt a little awkward and embarrassed.

'You know why we're here?' Sue asked.

'Yes, the police told me.' Lucy avoided saying Dugdale's name in case she gave away her feelings about him. 'Are you going to help?' she asked.

'Apparently this Vita'll get away with it if this doesn't come off. It's rather an eccentric trick for the police to pull but I suppose it's worth a try, isn't it?'

'Oh, yes,' Lucy said, and her eyes were shining.

'I've met Vita,' Sue said. 'I didn't realize at the time who she was, and I don't remember much about it now, but apparently I gave her my telephone number.'

'Did you really,' Lucy said, making something so simple sound exciting. 'Why?'

Sue looked surprised at the question. 'I've absolutely no idea,' she said.

They both laughed.

'Anyway,' Sue said, 'she knows about Paul and me because apparently I told her. So I'll ring her and ask her to come to my place to talk about Paul.'

'But doesn't she come from somewhere up north?' Lucy said. 'How would you know her telephone number in London?'

She's not quite as stupid as she looks, Sue told herself, she's just a bit simple. Maybe no professional business woman used to these things would ever have to ask that question, but it shows she's keeping up with the plot.

'That won't be a problem,' she said, 'If she asks, I'll tell her I got it out of someone at her club in Manchester. After all, they must have a contact for her.'

'I don't see why she'd come to talk to you about Paul,' Lucy said. 'If she killed him, I'd imagine that's the last thing she'd want to do.'

'I've thought of that,' Sue said. 'So I've worked out a plan. If I play my cards right, she'll come to talk about money. Apparently the police think she killed him to inherit his money as next of kin. I'll tell her that he left a will leaving it all to me, and I want to discuss what to do next. Something like that.'

'But Paul didn't have any money.'

Sue thought, almost affectionately, that no one could live with someone as literal-minded as this woman without wanting to hit her. No wonder Paul could only take a weekend at a time.

She said, 'She thinks he had money.' She looked a bit shame-faced. 'I told her he had,' she said. 'I made it up. Apparently.'

'Oh.' Lucy, who couldn't lie if she tried, didn't know what to say. 'I think you're being very brave,' she added.

There was a short silence. Then Sue looked at her watch.

'What's happened to Guy? I told him I hadn't got long.'

'Guy?'

'You know, Chief Inspector Dugdale. He said to call him Guy.'

Lucy didn't like hearing Sue call Dugdale by his first name. She felt that something intimate between herself and him had been violated, although she recalled Sue Stockland had only helped the police with their inquiries. Why should she even know the inves-tigating officer's name was Guy? Except, of course, that she'd have been bound to ask as he was so good-looking.

It doesn't mean anything, Lucy told herself, that's just his style, he fixes women with those dark eyes and makes out he's fascinated by anything they say and they think he's interested in them, not just in what they can tell him. Guy calling Sue by her first name, she thought to herself, would be part of it, he'd do it automatically. It's nothing to do with being close to her, or even liking her.

'It's like hospitals,' Sue said. She thought Lucy hadn't understood what she meant. She went on, 'They always use first names, makes it more friendly.'

'Less intimidating, yes,' Lucy said. 'I suppose the police do it to put suspects off their guard.'

'Suspects? But we're not suspects. He's just trying to be friendly.'

Lucy flushed, remembering that she had made Sue out to be a suspect.

Sue, seeing Lucy look embarrassed, thought, My God, she's remembering how I told Guy she killed Paul.

Lucy said, 'All this about Vita is a bit of a shock, to be honest. I kind of thought it was all sorted when they got that tattooed man.'

'Well,' Sue said, 'in the absence of our policeman friend, are we up for this?'

'We don't really have any choice, do we?' Lucy said. 'It's basic justice. If she did it, she should be punished.'

'And if she didn't, there's no harm done,' Sue said.

'So you'll ring her and set it up?'

'Yes. And I'll let you know the details.'

'So let me get this right, you'll get her to confess?' Lucy said.

'And you'll overhear what she says and tape it as evidence.'

'Do you think evidence like that is admissible?' Lucy asked.

'If we can make her confess she did it, the police will find the evidence,' Sue said.

Each was a little chilled by the way the other did not seem to find this disturbing.

'Suppose she doesn't confess?' Lucy said. 'They can't arrest her for visiting you.'

'If she doesn't confess, we abort everything and you just stay hidden until she leaves,' Sue said.

Lucy had the impression that Sue didn't intend that this should happen.

'Let's have another drink,' Lucy said. 'I don't see why Guy shouldn't pay for being so late.'

'I think we've managed rather well without him,' Sue said.

She signalled to a waiter, who brought more drinks. The two women settled back in their chairs and Sue raised her glass.

'To the end of the affair,' she said.

Lucy hesitated, a little shocked at Sue's directness. Then she leaned forward and touched her glass to Sue's.

'And new beginnings,' she said.

Sue drank and then put her drink down on the table, giving Lucy a sideways look.

'Is it going well, your new beginning?' she asked.

'Well,' Lucy said, 'it's early days, but yes, I think perhaps it is. What about you?'

Lucy saw Sue's face soften as she said, 'There is someone I really like. I'm keeping my fingers crossed.'

'I'm so confused,' Lucy said, 'I thought Paul was the only man there could ever be for me, and then wham! he's killed, and before I even have time to know how devastated I feel, I find myself falling in love with someone else.'

'Perhaps that's what happens when you lose someone like that,' Sue said. 'It's exactly the same for me, it's almost as though Paul never existed.'

'I know,' Lucy said. 'I felt bad about that at first. But I think it's because he wasn't the person I thought he was. First I felt betrayed, and then stupid. Then it was as though I'd never really known him at all and I blamed myself. Did you feel that?'

'Yes, pretty much exactly. I thought I was the only one who would react like that, that there was something wrong with me. I'm glad you feel the same, now I don't feel so damn guilty.'

Lucy wanted to say something more, but before they could settle down to swap confidences, Sue's mobile rang. With a shrug of apology, she answered it.

'I don't know what I can do about it,' she said, 'I don't speak Estonian. Tell him to hire an interpreter.'

There were sounds like squawking on the line.

'OK,' Sue said, nearly shouting to make herself heard. 'I'll come now.'

She put the phone back in her handbag, then stood up.

'I'm sorry,' she said, 'duty calls.'

'I take it that's nothing to do with new beginnings?' Lucy said.

'God, no,' Sue said. 'It would be like being in love with a grizzly bear. We'll be in touch about the Vita thing. See you then.'

Lucy stood up. She wasn't sure what she should do, air kiss that porcelain cheek, or shake hands. She did neither, but sat down again.

Sue hurried out, obviously preoccupied with her Estonian problem.

Lucy finished her drink and was wondering if she should stay or try to contact Guy later when Dugdale rushed into the bar, looking flustered.

'I'm so sorry,' he said. 'Something I had to deal with. Has Sue gone already, or didn't she come?'

'She had to leave,' Lucy said. 'We talked about it. She's going to fix things and she'll let you know.'

She put up her face to be kissed.

'Now,' she said, 'we can forget all that for a while, can't we? At least I've got you all to myself for a few hours.'

31 Setting the Trap

Dugdale finished his phone call and sat back to meet Malone's accusing eye.

Malone looked for signs that his boss was having doubts about pursuing what seemed to him a mad scheme. But all he detected was a certain suppressed excitement.

'It's on for this evening,' Dugdale said.

He obviously didn't feel he needed to explain to Malone which of their many ongoing cases he was talking about.

'Are you sure about this, sir?'

'Lighten up, Sergeant,' Dugdale said. 'The only thing that can go wrong now is if this woman Vita didn't do it. But she did.'

'This is highly irregular,' Malone said.

'Well, being regular hasn't got us a result yet, has it?'

'We had a cut and dried result with Jed Mallet,' Malone said, 'except that wasn't good enough for you.'

Dugdale looked at him with genuine curiosity. 'So you'd have been happy to let it go at that and the real killer get away with it?'

Malone shuffled his feet.

'Of course not,' he said. 'If she did it….'

He saw Dugdale draw breath to start convincing him of why he thought he had a case, and quickly added, 'It's OK, you've convinced me. If it makes you feel better, I think she did it, too. And I'm behind you a hundred percent. All I wish is that we didn't have to involve civilians.'

'I know,' Dugdale said, 'but I couldn't see a way round it, and I still can't.'

'So what's the plan of action?'

'It's all set up. Sue ... Ms Stockland ... has arranged with the doorman to let us wait in the empty flat next door to hers. Apparently the fellow thinks she saved his life when Mallet attacked him and he can't do enough for her. God knows what he thinks she's up to, hiding men in one flat while she's with someone else in her own....'

'Perhaps we should take a woman officer with us,' Malone said.

'The fewer people who know anything about this the better,' Dugdale said. 'We don't want to broadcast what we're up to.'

'We're agreed on that,' Malone said, 'when this operation goes pear-shaped, can we keep it to ourselves?'

Dugdale pretended to ignore him. 'Stockland's flat has a folding door between the sitting-room and the bedroom,' he said, 'so that'll be closed and Lucy Drake will hide there with her tape recorder. She'll hear everything.'

'Why does she have to be involved? Surely we could cover everything without her? We could set up a hidden tape recorder in the room and record what's said.'

'We're dealing with a killer, Derek. Get that into your head. Vita's not just a bad-tempered loudmouth. If she found the tape, the whole operation would be blown. And anyway, when the time comes, I'd like two of them standing up in court as witnesses for the prosecution. It's more difficult to gag two than one, if you get my meaning?'

'I suppose so.'

'And Lucy will be on hand if things turn nasty.'

'I hope you're not going to tell me that you picked her up specifically for this job because she's a fine big girl for fighting?' Malone said.

Dugdale looked aghast, then decided that this must be one of Malone's attempts at a joke. He grinned.

'Horses for courses, Derek, our girls are both tough cookies in their own way, but in this they're up against a real pro.'

'I wonder if those two young women realize what a friend they've found in you,' Malone said, with no attempt to hide his sarcasm.

32 A Hunt to the Death

L ucy sat on the end of Sue Stockland's bed. The light in the room was fading. Guy Dugdale had told them not to put on a light in the bedroom. Vita might be watching from outside and she might smell a trap if she could see Sue moving about in the sitting-room when there was also a light on in the bedroom.

Lucy was so nervous that she had lost her sense of time, and she wondered how long she had been waiting; it was too dark now to read her watch. She felt very anxious. Partly because of where she was – in the bedroom that Paul had shared with Sue. Both of them had been acutely aware of this when Sue showed her into the room, but they had carefully avoided mentioning Paul's name.

Mostly it was fearful anticipation which caused the butterflies in Lucy's stomach, her shaking hands and dry mouth. She was both dreading and looking forward to the moment when Vita stepped into the flat and the game began in earnest.

There was a light under the door from the sitting-room where Sue was waiting. Lucy could hear her moving about. She'd been told to do that and to keep as close to the window as possible so that Vita could see her from the street if she was watching. Sue probably feels worse than I do, Lucy thought, I've only got to stay here and listen, but Vita's confession, her future conviction and punishment, all depend on Sue.

I'm glad she is the one in there, Lucy told herself. I couldn't carry it off. But Sue can. She's a hunter by nature, an aggressive predator, while I'm not. I'd rather run than fight.

And then she wondered: where would I draw the line if I had to? If I'd known about Sue and Paul, would I have fought for him, or just let it go? How did Sue react when she found out about me? Will I ever really be able to talk to her about it?

And then she thought, I'm glad actually, that if Paul had to die as he did, Sue and I didn't find out about each other sooner. Sue's tougher than me, she'd have found a way to stop him seeing me. She'd have got him away from me. Or me away from him. And then I might never have got over him.

Lucy didn't speculate on how Sue would have done this; she was simply certain that her rival would have been ruthless.

What am I doing? she asked herself, speculating about things that never happened when I should be concentrating on what's happening here and now.

Thank God it isn't me facing Vita, she thought again, I'm not sure I could do it, entrapping another woman whom Paul must've loved once and who'd loved him.

She told herself that she was only helping out, she'd be the witness in court when Vita was on trial for killing Paul. I'm not alone, she thought, Guy and Malone are in the flat next door. If anything goes wrong, they'll be on hand. Or will they? Suddenly the flat next door seemed a long way away.

There was a sharp ring at the front door. Lucy heard Sue move to answer it. She took up her position beside the closed partition between the rooms and pressed the record button of the tape recorder on the floor beside her.

Oh God, she thought, what happens if the tape runs out. She'll hear me changing it.

Then she reminded herself that she'd put in a new tape. I've got two hours recording time; the tape will automatically reverse at the end of an hour. I've nothing to worry about on that score. I'm making things worse for myself. All I've got to do is keep out of sight and listen. I'm not in any danger, it's Sue who's in danger.

But it was no good, she could not calm her fears. She sat cross-legged on the floor of the darkening room and was afraid that rather than Vita's confession the deafening beating of her heart would be the only sound that anyone would hear on the tape recorder.

But suppose I sneeze? she thought, suppose my stomach makes a noise and Vita guesses she's walked into a trap. She'll kill Sue. Will I be able to stop her? Or will she kill me as well?

Lucy made a huge effort to pull herself together. She concentrated on listening.

Vita's voice was harsh. But that, Lucy thought, was her Northern accent, not a sign that she, too, was nervous.

'Nice place you've got,' Vita was saying, 'was it Paul's?'

She sounded tough, tough and aggressive. Sue would see her blunt question as a threat, Lucy was sure of that. The implication was that if the place was Paul's, Sue could take it that she was under notice to quit. Bad move, Vita, Lucy thought, that's the way to make Sue angry.

But she heard no trace of anger in Sue's reply.

'No,' Sue said, 'it's mine. Paul lived here with me.'

Vita didn't say anything, but Lucy had no doubt that she thought Sue was lying.

'Have a drink,' Sue said.

'Scotch,' Vita said. 'Neat.'

There was a clinking of glasses.

'Well?' Vita said. 'You haven't got me up here to talk about the weather. What do you want to say? Am I going to get what's owed to me, or are you going to cause trouble?'

Sue didn't reply at once. Lucy manoeuvred herself to a kneeling position so that if she put her eye to the crack between the folding doors, she had a very narrow view of Vita.

She glimpsed her profile, and then one over-mascara-ed eye

which was so black that the pale-blue iris looked white. Vita's large breasts bulged out of a black lace top. Lucy, as always in jeans and rollneck sweater, was shocked that anyone associated with Paul could walk around in public like that. Vita looked like a tart. But then, Lucy thought, she was a tart and he knew that when he married her.

As so often in the short weeks since Paul died, Lucy wondered how the man she thought she knew could be so different from the actual person she was now discovering.

Stop it, she told herself, there's no point.

She leaned forward again to peer through the crack in the door.

Sue was sitting on the sofa close to Vita. She must be trying to make sure that Vita didn't do anything behind her back.

'Are you really Paul's wife?' Sue asked.

'Oh, yes,' Vita said. 'And I've got the papers to prove it. We were never divorced, so don't come that "this is my flat" stuff with me. Everything he had is mine.'

'Except he didn't have anything,' Sue said.

Vita's laugh was not pleasant. 'Pull the other one,' she said, 'you told me yourself how rich he was, when you were drunk in my bar.'

'I know I did,' Sue said. 'I don't know how I got so drunk that night.'

'Who cares?' Vita said. 'You showed me his picture, you called him your rich and successful boyfriend. When you showed me his picture, I couldn't believe it was my own Paul you were talking about.'

'So when you heard he was murdered, you thought you'd come and claim your inheritance, right?' Sue said.

'No, I came before I heard he was dead. Serendipitous, wasn't it?'

'Paul dying, you mean?'

Sue got up and took Vita's glass to fill it. Lucy saw Vita lean forward. She moved Sue's glass, which was still half full, out of Lucy's sight.

'Oh,' said Vita airily when Sue sat down again, 'that wasn't serendipity.'

'Are you saying you killed him yourself?'

Lucy admired Sue. She sounded so cool. She might have been talking about the weather, not about the man she'd loved.

'Now I didn't say that, did I?' Vita said, with a grotesque archness. 'He was my husband, I've got my rights. I came down to claim them. He had to support me. But I won't pretend, him dying will save me the trouble of a fight to get him to see it that way.'

'And so you thought how much more you'd get out of him if he died and you inherited everything, right?'

'That's the law. I'm his next of kin.'

'That might be true if he died intestate,' Sue said. 'Except he left a will.'

'He what?' Vita said.

Her eyes narrowed. She certainly hadn't expected this.

'He'd made a will,' Sue said. 'He left everything to me.'

'You're lying,' Vita said.

Lucy was shocked at the malice in her tone as Vita hissed at Sue: 'You're lying. What's your game?'

'I'll show you.' Sue disappeared, then came back and handed Vita a brown envelope. 'It's all in there,' she said.

Vita didn't open the envelope. What's in it? Lucy wondered. This wasn't part of the plan. And then she remembered Sue saying she'd think of something to sound convincing. But, she thought, isn't she playing a dangerous game? Paul didn't write a will. Whatever's in that envelope, it isn't a legal will. Why should he make a will? He had nothing to leave.

'This is Paul's will?' Vita sounded shocked; and unsure, as though she was trying to stall Sue while she thought of what to do next.

Sue didn't answer. She probably nodded, Lucy thought.

'I need another drink,' Vita said. She was still stalling.

Vita pushed her glass across the table. Lucy saw Sue's hand pick it up. Sue's own glass, still half-full, suddenly appeared in the centre of the table, as though Sue had pushed it back from the edge when she took Vita's for a refill. Vita started to search her handbag. She took out a packet of cigarettes and took one out to smoke.

'Where's the ashtray?' she said.

'This must come as quite a shock for you,' Sue said as she put down a full glass of whisky in front of Vita.

Vita looked up, apparently watching Sue's face. Lucy could see that her expression was wary, that she recognized Sue was her enemy.

But Sue went on as though she had noticed nothing. 'I mean,' she said, 'you go to all that trouble setting everything up, whether or not you sort of nudged fate, if you know what I mean, and now you find out it was all a waste of time. I'd feel pretty bitter myself.'

Vita smiled. 'Paul would have told me if he'd made a will. He wasn't the sort to make a will, he thought he'd never die,' she said. 'This is a scam.'

'But you didn't see him before he died, did you, so he couldn't tell you? You and I both know you were in Manchester the night before, and you didn't know if he was alive or dead then. Not till you saw the photo I showed you. I tell you, I looked everywhere for him the night after, the night he died, and you weren't anywhere I went.'

Vita shrugged. 'So what? I didn't see him, I talked to him on his mobile.'

'No you didn't,' Sue said. She sounded almost bored. 'His mobile was in his office, he didn't have it on him.'

Vita put her lighted cigarette on the edge of the table so that the ash would fall on the carpet and took a compact out of her handbag and started to repair her make-up.

Sue picked up the glowing stub and walked off with it. Lucy leaned back on her heels to ease the pressure on her knees. She put her eye back to her crack when she heard Sue's voice again.

'You must've really wanted money, Vita, to come looking for someone you'd forgotten all about.'

'I see what you're after,' Vita said, as though she was working something out in her head. 'You're playing with fire. If Paul really left everything to you in a proper will, you could have killed him yourself. If I tell the police about it, they could easily arrest you. You wouldn't hesitate to kill him, would you? You're a hard-faced little bitch, I can tell that. But perhaps not, perhaps a bloody little princess like you hasn't got the nerve....'

Vita's voice suddenly sounded funny, like somebody who's been to the dentist before the novocaine has worn off.

Lucy expected Sue to say something really cutting after that. I'd give her a good slap for saying something like that, she told herself, but Sue seemed content to let it go. Perhaps she's right, Lucy thought, she's treating it with the contempt it deserves.

Then Sue said, 'But the police aren't after me. You're the suspect. So let's see, how did you kill him? You can't fool me, all you club people know all about drugs, don't you? You wouldn't have had any trouble getting hold of heroin, would you? Neville told me all about people like you. He used to be a junkie, poor Neville. Go on, you tell me how you did it.'

There was no excitement or emotion in Sue's voice at all. She's putting on a tremendous show, Lucy thought, much better than I could ever have done. I'd have given the game away by now.

Sue went on, 'You spiked his drink, didn't you, and he thought he was just drunk? It was funny, he couldn't stand up or anything, but he kept on about how he'd got to get to the car because Lucy would be waiting for him. Isn't that right, Vita, isn't that how it was?'

Sue made a sound which Lucy took to be a cross between

encouraging Vita to continue and jealousy because Paul had been thinking of Lucy.

'Come on, Vita, tell me that's what happened,' she said.

Sue seemed to be dragging the words out from somewhere deep inside herself.

She did love Paul, Lucy said to herself, she can hardly speak, she's so emotional.

Sue's voice sounded thick with tears as she went on. 'You helped him down to the car and then you injected the heroin and put the syringe in his hand. Didn't you?'

'You're crazy,' Vita said, sounding muffled.

There was a crash, then a scuffling sound.

My God, Lucy thought, they're fighting.

She hesitated, not sure what to do. This wasn't what was supposed to happen. Lucy was afraid that if she burst in on the two women, she would ruin Guy's careful plan.

Then something flashed across Lucy's line of vision. She saw a syringe poised, then four arms raised, hands trying to wrest it away.

There was banging outside the room, then there were people in the room, blocking Lucy's view of Sue and Vita.

Someone screamed, Sue or Vita; men shouted; something – a vase or lamp – smashed on the floor.

Then the noise ceased as suddenly as it had started.

Lucy opened the bedroom door and surveyed the scene.

Sue seemed to be slumped on the floor behind the sofa. There was a gurgling sound which might or might not be coming from her. Vita lay across the sofa. She looked as though she was sleeping, snoring slightly. Dugdale was leaning over Sue. Malone, beside Vita, was on his mobile calling for an ambulance. It seemed to Lucy that almost at once there were policemen bustling about as though they weren't sure what they should be doing.

Lucy went across to the group round the sofa. She couldn't see

Sue's face, only her feet in a pair of absurdly frivolous shoes, shoes which looked enormous and ridiculous.

'Sue,' Lucy said, 'what happened? Are you OK?'

Guy Dugdale got to his feet and led Lucy away.

'Is she dead?' she asked him. 'What happened?'

An ambulance crew arrived. The police officers moved out of the way to let them get to work.

'I'll explain later,' Dugdale said to Lucy. 'Wait for me in the bedroom, will you? It shouldn't take too long to clear up here.'

Malone came up to Dugdale. 'They're about to take them to the hospital. What do you want me to do.'

'Go there with them, and when she comes round, charge her with Paul Meyer's murder,' Dugdale said. 'We've got all we need now.'

33 A Pawn in the Game

Lucy felt she had been waiting for hours. At first there'd been sounds of activity in the sitting-room next door, but then everything seemed to go silent. But Guy had asked her to wait there, and wait she would. At least she could have the light on now.

Rather than sit on the bed that Sue had shared with Paul, Lucy had perched herself on a decorative bedroom chair covered in some slippery material which made it hard not to slide to the floor if she tried to relax. But she must have fallen asleep because when she got stiffly to her feet and stumbled to the window, it was broad daylight outside. The streets below were busy with people hurrying this way and that, aimlessly as far as she could see. A deafening noise came from the traffic on a main road that she could make out beyond traffic lights at the end of a street which was lined with parked cars.

How can anyone live in a place like this? Lucy asked herself, how can they bear that noise all the time?

She turned back into the room.

She couldn't rid herself of the thought that Paul had slept there with Sue. She began to explore the room for signs that he had been at home there.

Everything visible was Sue's – her cosmetics and hairbrush on the dressing-table; costume jewellery spilling out of a box beside the mirror; a hair dryer plugged into the socket under the window.

Lucy opened the doors of the built-in wardrobes. Sue's clothes only, none of Paul's. He might never have existed in this room. Lucy wondered if Sue had packed everything away the day after he died and given it to a charity shop. Lucy was impressed and also depressed by Sue's efficiency in eradicating every trace of the man she was supposed to have loved. She must be tough, Lucy thought, I couldn't be that cold-blooded. She must've hated him for what he did to her. And then she said to herself, I did the same thing, unintentionally. Everything got cleared out the next day, because I had to move out in a hurry. But if the builders hadn't been moving in at once, Paul's things would have been lying around for ages. I couldn't have thrown them out. I don't know how Sue could do it. She *is* weird.

Lucy opened another door and found herself confronting a wall of shelves covered in pairs of women's shoes. Leather shoes, silk and velvet shoes, shoes of every conceivable colour trimmed with ribbon or sparkling buckles and straps, shoes with stiletto heels, metal heels, flat heels. And yet there was some-thing odd about these shoes. Lucy picked up a pair, then another. They were far too big for a woman to wear.

'What are you doing?' Guy's voice behind her made Lucy jump.

'Nothing,' she said, then added, 'I'm sorry, I was looking for any signs that Paul ever lived here.'

Lucy felt too ashamed to lie.

'Poor Lucy.' Dugdale looked embarrassed, clearly not sure what he should say.

'That's all in the past now,' Lucy said. 'Tell me what's been happening. Is Sue all right? And Vita?'

'We've charged her with Paul's murder. She'll be sent for trial as soon as she's fit enough to go to court.'

'Thank God for that,' Lucy said. 'The woman's a monster. I saw her face as she went to attack Sue and I'll never forget it, those eyes, no one who saw her eyes could doubt Vita was a killer.'

'Vita?' Dugdale said, sounding surprised. 'Not Vita. Sue murdered Paul.'

Lucy felt the room spin and she sat down suddenly on the edge of the bed.

'Sue?' she said. 'What do you mean, Sue?'

Dugdale sat down beside her and put his arm round her shoulders.

'I'm sorry,' he said, 'I thought you understood. When Sue said Vita couldn't have talked to Paul on his mobile the night he died, because it was in his office, I thought you'd realize then that she must've been in his office herself to know that. We found the phone there.'

'No,' Lucy said, 'no, I didn't think anything of it at all. But I heard Vita confess, for God's sake.'

'No, what you actually heard was Sue telling her what the story was going to be. Not that Vita would be around to deny it.'

'But Vita isn't dead. Is she?'

'No, no, she got a hefty dose of Rohypnol, that's all. She's sleeping it off.'

'Rohypnol?'

'It's a knockout drug. It's what they use for date rape. Sue gave it to Paul, too, before she injected him with the heroin overdose that killed him,' Dugdale said. 'She'd have done the same to Vita.'

'I saw a syringe,' Lucy said, 'but I thought Vita was trying to kill Sue.' She paused, then frowned and added, 'This is daft, Guy, you must have got it wrong. Sue's the one who got hurt. If she was the killer, how did she end up nearly dead?'

Dugdale nodded. 'Vita was on her guard when Sue wanted to see her. We may have suspected Vita, but Vita herself knew she didn't do it. Actually, I don't think it occurred to her that Sue might've killed Paul, either. She probably thought that was down to some sort of Big Saul gang business. So she didn't think Sue was going to kill her – anyway not until she began to feel the effects of the Rohypnol. But once she did – and Vita's used to drugs – she'd know what that meant. So, when Sue brought out her lethal syringe, Vita fought back. Vita's a toughie, and it was Sue who got the knock-out dose of heroin, not Vita.'

'Is Sue going to make it?'

'It's touch and go. It was a massive dose. But if she does, she's going away for a long time. There's not just Paul's murder, there's deadly assault at least on Vita, if not attempted murder.'

Lucy shook her head. 'I can't believe it. She and I both slept with Paul, that makes us practically related.'

Dugdale looked at her with an odd expression.

'Yes,' he said, 'I think I know how you must feel.'

Lucy smiled at him, grateful to him for making an effort to be understanding.

'But why? Why did she kill him? She loved him, I'm sure she did. As much as I did.'

Dugdale shrugged. 'I think that's partly why. If you ask me, a lot of men had loved Sue Stockland, but Paul was the first she loved. She couldn't bear it that she loved him more than he loved her. I got the impression, talking to her about him, that she was always quite insecure about their relationship. And then she found out about you.'

'Well, I found out about her. It never occurred to me to murder him.'

'It was the money which drove Sue over the top, I think. He hadn't really loved her, but worse still she realized he'd only been interested in her for the money. She'd see that as a declaration of war.'

Lucy shook her head. She looked around Sue's room, at her things, the cosmetics on the dressing-table, the purple-patterned duvet on the bed, the paperback book on the bedside table.

'What kind of monster is she?' she said. 'You'd never think she could be like that. She had a successful business, she was gorgeous to look at, she'd got this flat and everything she wanted. How did she even get hold of heroin?'

'That dress designer friend of hers, Neville, used to be a junkie. We looked into his records and he got the stuff through some crooked Estonian businessmen. It turns out one of the Estonians is a client of Sue's. Perhaps she got it through him, but anyway, even if Neville had cleaned up his act, a lot of his friends hadn't. It may well have been lying around in his flat. Sue spent a lot of time with him. I don't know exactly how she got it, but it wouldn't have been difficult.'

'But Guy, what possessed her? She knew you were only yards away. She knew I was in there listening, getting it all down on tape. We did get it all on tape?'

'Yes, we checked it, but it's inconclusive. Remember, you heard everything and you thought Sue'd led Vita into confessing. That's what anyone who hears the tape and doesn't know Sue was the murderer would think.'

'But—'

'Yes.' Dugdale took Lucy's hand and pressed it. 'Yes, you'd know, of course you'd know she was the murderer. She'd have had to kill you, too, wouldn't she?'

'But suppose she had, what would she have done then? How could she explain me and Vita, both of us dead under her nose? You and Malone were only next door.'

'She had the nerve of the devil.' He couldn't hide a note almost of admiration in his voice. 'She'd got that covered. She'd not only dosed Vita with Rohypnol, she took it herself as part of her cover. She got a bit too clever for her own good, though. That's probably why Vita was able to fight back so effectively. Sue hadn't quite timed it right, and the stuff worked quicker than she'd expected. Sue's plan was to inject Vita, hit you over the head, and pass out before we barged in.'

'She must be crazy,' Lucy said.

'She'd one thing going for her,' Dugdale said, 'she thought we were out to get Vita, so as far as we knew she was innocent. She banked on that.'

'She was taking a hell of a risk,' Lucy said. 'Poor Sue,' she added and then she thought how soft that was, feeling sorry for a woman who was going to kill you.

'She'd have been clear and free, though, if it had come off. We'd have had Vita down for it without a doubt.'

Lucy thought that Dugdale looked embarrassed. He must be feeling guilty he got it so wrong about Vita, she thought. And she added to herself, he thinks I'm going to say 'I told you so.' I told him Sue killed Paul but he didn't listen. No wonder he's embarrassed.

Dugdale said, 'Presumably she relied on us taking it for granted that Vita had drugged her, killed you, and then, finding you'd taped everything and she was trapped, committed suicide rather than be caught. It may sound far-fetched, but it would be very hard to disprove. Especially because Sue would be the only witness and would tell us her version of what happened. She nearly pulled it off; she would have if she hadn't underestimated what a tough old bird Vita is.'

'Sue underestimated you, too, didn't she? But at least I know you saved my life. I'd be dead by now if it wasn't for you, Guy.'

Dugdale looked really embarrassed now.

'Malone thinks what I did was very unprofessional. I risked your life as a means to an end and he thinks that was wrong.'

'God,' Lucy said, 'you must be relieved at the way things turned out. You set a trap for Vita and you end up getting the real murderer. It might have been disastrous.'

'I thought on balance you wouldn't mind when it meant catching Paul's killer.'

For the first time the enormity of what might have happened hit home. Lucy shuddered and got up.

'Guy, if you don't mind I think I'm going to go straight to Paddington to get a train home. I want to get away from here, this place gives me the creeps.'

For a moment, she was afraid that Guy was going to take her

in his arms and make love to her there, on the bed Sue had shared with Paul. He might think she was looking for something like that to comfort her and if he did, she didn't think she could bear ever to see him again.

But he didn't.

'Of course,' he said, 'I'll get someone to drive you to the station. You go home and be with your friends and try to forget about this. I'll ring you tomorrow.'

He gave her a quick peck on the forehead as he went out.

34 Male Intuition

Malone was in the empty flat next to Sue Stockdale's where the doorman, Ted, had let them set up their operation. He was clearing away cigarette butts and polystyrene coffee cups when Dugdale walked in.

'What did she say?' Malone asked.

'What did who say about what?' Dugdale said snappishly.

Malone said nothing. After a while, Dugdale picked up a full ashtray, opened the window, and threw the butts out.

'I didn't exactly tell her,' he said. 'What would've been the point?'

'So she still thinks we set up that whole scam to trap Vita into confessing?'

'Yes, I suppose she does. So Lucy Drake thinks we made a mistake and then struck lucky? It doesn't make much difference, does it?'

'She might've felt differently about setting Sue Stockland up.'

'She might,' Dugdale agreed, 'she might have refused to do it. We needed her. We had to have someone to back up Vita's story about what happened in there, and we've got that.'

'She's got a right to know you used her.'

'She does know I used her. I told her that before we set up the operation,' Dugdale said. 'If I'd told her I was after Sue, she'd have given the game away. Lucy is the world's worst liar.'

'But you knew all the time you were after Sue Stockland, not Vita. You should tell her that.'

'Be honest, Derek, aren't you really pissed off because I didn't tell *you* until the last moment? Isn't it really you who'd have backed out if I'd told you what I suspected?'

'It was a stupid risk to take. If the Stockland woman was the killer, you knew she'd have to silence Lucy Drake as well as Vita.'

'There wasn't any other way, Derek. Be honest, was there? Sue would never have fallen for a set-up like that if she hadn't thought that by marking Vita as the killer she'd be letting herself off the hook for good and all.'

'What if it had gone wrong and Vita or Lucy Drake had been killed? How would you have dealt with that?'

Malone's tone was still critical, but he sounded curious, too.

Dugdale had no adequate answer to the question. He deliberately sounded heartless enough to silence Malone's questions.

'We'd have had what even those sods at the CPS couldn't deny was a body of evidence,' he said.

'I'm glad I don't have a mind like yours,' Malone muttered. 'And I'm more than glad I'm not a woman who thinks you're in love with her.'

Dugdale raised an eyebrow in the way he had which infuriated Malone, and the sergeant had no come-back.

'Will you admit that the way things worked out you're glad I didn't tell you what I had in mind?' Dugdale said. 'At least we've got a good result which won't do your career any more harm than it'll do mine.'

'I'm glad you didn't tell me, because I'd never have believed we could pull it off,' Malone said. 'Sir,' he added.

Dugdale couldn't think of anything to say. He felt tired, and oddly troubled by what Lucy had said about how she felt involved in Sue's crime because they had both slept with Paul. He and Paul had both made love to Sue, what was he to make of that?

'I may have reservations about your methods in this case,'

Malone said after a while, 'and I think you took a stupid risk. But since it came off, are you going to let me in on the secret? How the hell did you know it was Sue Stockland we were after?'

'It was such a silly little thing,' Dugdale said. 'Just that she said once at the start of this that she'd left messages on Meyer's mobile about meeting him to give him the money she had for him.'

Malone looked puzzled. 'And—?' he said.

'Well, she didn't, did she?' Dugdale said. 'I went through his mobile and the phone in his office and at Stockland's flat and she never left a message anywhere. And yet she was desperate to see him that night. She left messages all right, from Manchester, for a start, to tell him she couldn't meet him with the money. She even rang Lucy looking for him. Maybe, I thought to myself, she wiped the messages. And in that case she must've been in his office that night because that's where his mobile was. I found it there, didn't I? With no messages and no incoming calls from Manchester. Nothing much at all except a few business contacts and Lucy Drake's telephone number.'

'You'd expect that, wouldn't you?'

'But Sue Stockland wouldn't have, would she? That could've been the first time she'd seen it. That could've been when she made her first call to Lucy with that rigmarole about Paul's wife telling her to ring 1471 on his private telephone and ring her.'

'You mean—?' Malone looked puzzled.

'Well, Sue had to explain how she'd got Lucy's number when she rang to find out if Paul was two-timing her, didn't she? Dialling 1471's a bloody hit-and-miss system for something as crucial as that. You can't be sure that the one you want's the last call on the line.

Malone shook his head in bewilderment. 'She should have been a lawyer,' he said. 'And she seemed such a nice young woman to meet.'

The telephone rang, and Malone answered it. He listened for a moment, then replaced the receiver.

'We were lucky Paul Meyer owed Kramer so much money,' Malone said. 'If that hadn't been a factor in Meyer's murder, it would've been stretching the bounds of legality too far to force Kramer's accountant to disclose his financial records....'

'... And it was all there in black and white,' Malone finished happily.

They grinned at each other.

'We've got him exactly where we want him now,' Dugdale said, 'money laundering and tax evasion. He's going down on those charges. And best of all, every crooked penny will almost certainly be confiscated by the government. Maybe it'll go towards a beleaguered police force. Rough justice, eh? But justice all the same.'

'It's made a difference to the unsolved crimes files,' Malone said. 'Closing this case has tied up quite a few loose ends.'

'You did well,' Dugdale said, 'go on home before something else happens here to keep you from your family. Give Mrs Malone a surprise – unless she's out at one of her classes?'

'No, she's in tonight,' Malone said, 'I'll give her a ring to tell her I'll be early. What are you doing yourself?'

Dugdale realized that this was a surreptitious invitation, made out of a kind of embarrassment because he was on his own. He wished sometimes that he could go down to the pub with the others and buy a round after a successful case, but not drinking made it difficult to enter into the team spirit. Malone was half-suggesting that Dugdale should spend the evening at his home and Dugdale appreciated it, but he also knew that he, Malone, and Malone's wife, would hate every moment of it.

'Me? Oh, I've got a date tonight,' Dugdale said. 'I'm all right.'

Malone watched him walk away down the corridor to the lift. He thought his boss was lying about his date, and if so, he understood why. Dugdale made people feel awkward when he tried to meet them socially, and Malone was sure he was conscious of that. He was best on his own. Unless, of course, he was spending the evening with Lucy Drake. Except that she'd been driven to Paddington Station to catch a train back to her West Country cloud-cuckoo-land, so the date wasn't with her.

The phone on Dugdale's desk began to ring. Malone thought of ignoring it, but he couldn't. He picked up the receiver.

'Chief Inspector's phone,' he said.

'Is he there?'

Malone recognized Lucy's voice.

'No,' Malone said, 'he's left for the night, I think. Can I help?'

There was a pause, then Lucy said, 'There's something I've got to know, Sergeant, and you can probably tell me. Did Guy know beforehand that he was laying a trap for Sue Stockland, not Vita?'

Malone thought of saying that she should ask Dugdale that question, not him. But then he thought, This is unfair, she deserves to be told.

'Yes,' he said, and then, hoping to soften the blow, added, 'we both knew.'

'Thank you for telling me the truth,' Lucy said, 'and thank you for lying, too.'

Malone heard himself saying, 'And there's something else I think you should know. He was sleeping with Sue Stockland.'

My God, he thought, what made me tell her that? I didn't mean to say that.

There was a short silence. Malone was trying to think of something explanatory to say and then all he could hear was the dialling tone.

He walked across the office to the window, vaguely thinking that if he saw Dugdale in the car park he could hail him and tell him about Lucy's call. I should warn him, Malone thought, guiltily aware that he had been disloyal to his boss.

He saw Dugdale among a group of people emerging from the station entrance. He was about to open the window to shout when he realized that the chief was not alone. He and Vita Meyer walked together across the forecourt to the road. As Malone watched, Dugdale hailed a taxi and the two of them got in.

Malone watched the taxi until it was lost in a stream of traffic at the road junction.

'So he did have a date,' Malone said aloud, 'the dirty bastard.'

He left the office feeling glad about what he had said to Lucy Drake.

35 Thank God It's Friday

It was Friday evening, Lucy's first in the thatched cottage by the village church which was her new home.

She loved the place already. After the vast dilapidated spaces in the old family home, the cottage seemed to settle comfortably round her, warm and welcoming. It was cosy, a place where pot plants flourished on the wide windowsills, and the smell of the climbing roses outside the windows filled the rooms through the open windows.

She had a cassoulet in the oven. It's becoming my standard dish for not spoiling while I wait for people to come, she thought.

And then she asked herself, How can I have been such an idiot about Paul? All those hours I wasted waiting for him, thinking I couldn't live without him.

Lucy smiled to herself, thinking about Paul without bitterness, only affection. I'd never be as happy as I am now, she thought, and then felt ashamed. But also excited. It's time to ring Guy, she told herself.

She dialled his mobile number and as she listened to the ringing tone she imagined him in his office with the sound of traffic through the open window, and the hot London summer air thick in the stifling room.

He answered the phone. 'Dugdale,' he said, and his name as he said it sounded like a snarl.

'Guy, it's Lucy.'

His voice changed as though the sound of her voice had transported him to a cool evening twilight in the country with the sound of running water and the chiming of the church clock.

'I'm still hard at it,' he said. 'I don't know when I'll get away.'

'That's what I'm ringing about, Guy,' Lucy said. 'I don't want you to come.'

'I will, as soon as I can get away,' Dugdale said, as though he was speaking a formula.

'No, you don't understand. It's not you, I loved being with you, but moving in here properly at last, I don't want anything bringing the taint of what happened into this place. I want to start again.'

'Lucy, I can't talk now. I'll see you later and then you can explain....'

'I know you were sleeping with Sue Stockland,' Lucy said. 'I've thought about that and I've decided that in the context of our affair, it's none of my business. But it's cleared my mind. You and I only existed because of what happened with Paul and then Sue, it was never going to survive once you'd solved the case.'

At last, Guy said, 'You're sure about this?'

Lucy could tell from his tone that Guy had been wondering how he could tell her that he felt the same. He was only surprised that she had come out with it first.

'Yes, I'm sure,' she said. 'We had a great time and helped each other out of a bad patch. At least, you helped me. But we don't know each other at all, really, except that we've nothing in common.'

Dugdale knew from her voice that she meant what she said; there was no question of one last night together, or an occasional future meal. He was surprised by how relieved he felt. He hadn't acknowledged to himself till now how fond he was of Lucy and how much he didn't want to contaminate her world with his.

'You know I'm always here if you need me,' he said, 'have a happy life.'

'Oh, I will,' she said. 'I know how to now. Goodbye Guy.'

She smiled to herself as she put down the phone. She had her new home, her new job as a partner in Quentin's business, the new life that had grown from her old like shoots from a pruned rose to look forward to. She was aware of a subtle change in her place in the village, a warmer feeling of being part of things replacing the slight distance there'd been while she had been perceived as a superior remnant of an old order. Only now though, in saying goodbye to Guy, had she finally cut a kind of emotional umbilical cord with her own old self. For the first time in her life, she knew what it felt like to feel free.

Maxine, Tara and Quentin, who had spent the day helping her to move in, called to her from the terrace.

'Here's the sustenance for the horny-handed sons of toil.' Quentin came into the kitchen with a bottle of wine, looking for an opener.

'Here, take this cassoulet out to the table on the terrace,' Lucy said, handing him oven gloves. 'I'll do the wine and Tara and Max can come and get knives and forks.'

It was eight-thirty by the clock on the church tower which overlooked the garden. Quentin had been watering the flower-beds earlier and the sun set light to the drops of water on the grass and covered the lavender bushes which bordered the lawn with a scattering of bright spangles.

'This is heaven,' Lucy said, turning her face up to the setting sun.

'Listen to those birds,' Quentin said, 'did anything ever sound so full of joy.'

Lucy raised her glass of wine in a toast. 'To new beginnings,' she said.